SOME THINGS THAT
MEANT THE WORLD TO ME

a novel by
JOSHUA MOHR

TWO DOLLAR RADIO
Books too loud to ignore.

Published by the Two Dollar Radio Movement, 2009.
Copyright © 2009 by Joshua Mohr.
All rights reserved.

Cover and layout design by Two Dollar Radio.

ISBN: 978-0-9820151-1-7
Library of Congress Control Number: 2009901232

TWO DOLLAR RADIO
Books too loud to ignore.

www.TwoDollarRadio.com
twodollar@TwoDollarRadio.com

SOME THINGS THAT
MEANT THE WORLD TO ME

"It takes a lot of whiskey to make these nightmares go away."

Tom Waits

MAN OF THE HOUR

I'd like to brag about the night I saved a hooker's life. Like to tell you how quiet everything else in the world was while I helped her. This was in San Francisco. Late 2007. I'd been drinking in Damascus, which was painted entirely black – floor, walls, and ceiling. Being surrounded by all that darkness had this slowing effect on time, like a shunned astronaut meandering in space. It was a Wednesday night, seemed like any other, but that was the way my life worked, things appearing one way and then getting poisoned.

And I'll tell you about other things, too. We'll talk about the past: the drifting house, my mom, Letch, the sidewinders, Dr. Angel-Hair. There's no way around those things.

Me, Rhonda, the hero.

They doused me in drugs and doctors and words, so many words, trying to make me see some lukewarm world. But I didn't. I don't.

So listen to me.

I was unemployed again but the bartender at Damascus used to work at a restaurant where I was a line cook, so he let me drink for free. I sidled in about ten at night and sat down next to a guy in a bowler hat, who offered to buy me a warm beer. I accepted and he said, "I'm wearing a diaper," and smiled; his teeth looked like frozen ginger ale.

His name was Vern. People had tried to introduce me to him before, but those times he'd been in blackouts, yelling things like, "That's no way to talk to your commanding officer!" He drank warm beers because the cold ones made his ancient teeth ache. His brand of choice was Michelob, and the bartenders at Damascus always kept a warm stash for Vern.

"Why a diaper?" I said, a familiar buzz slithering through my hands. Sometimes they felt like maracas: hollowed out, something bouncing around inside the skin.

"Gotta be ready for anything," Vern said and paid for the warm ones. "Like war." He took his bowler hat off and set it on the bar. Vern must have been seventy. He was bald. The hair he didn't have on top of his head, he made up for with eyebrows, fierce tangles of curly hair, long and rolled like handlebar mustaches.

The bartender set the beers down and walked away to help someone else.

"You got a problem with my diaper, boy?" Vern said.

Just last week, I'd seen him spit warm beer in a man's face because the guy was wearing a Dead Kennedys shirt. "I know that's a band," Vern had said to him, "but those dead Kennedy brothers may have saved our country. Now we live in a hive of shit." That was when he spit on him. The guy was probably forty years younger than Vern, but he didn't do anything about it, didn't even answer. Wiped the beer out of his eyes and walked away. He, like the rest of us, assumed if Vern was nuts enough to act that way he must know some cagey ways to bring men down.

My hands weren't physically shaking, so maybe maracas didn't really describe them. Maybe they were more like bags of microwave popcorn, inflating with violence as the kernels exploded. Dr. Angel-Hair used to say that the buzzing hands were because of my disorders. That I'd had a dissociative fugue. That I suffered from depersonalization, but that name always felt phony. Wasn't it exactly the opposite? I wasn't depersonalized. I was more of a person. I felt more, never went an hour without my maracas writhing and jerking and thrumming.

Vern waited for me to respond, and when he realized I wasn't going to say anything he said, "That's a good little boy," spanking himself and holding his warm beer up between us. I extended mine, our bottles touching.

"The older the buck," he said, "the harder the horns."

We drank.

His eyes glazed over, mouth hanging open.

"Are you okay?" I said.

Vern twirled the long matted hairs of one of his eyebrows, didn't answer for a few seconds. "Am now. Look," he said and pointed at his crotch: "No leaks."

I didn't want to sit with him or his temper or the blaring ways he reminded me of Letch, good and bad. I thanked him for the warm one and went outside to smoke.

Only two drags into my cigarette and I heard some muffled gagging noises coming from down the block, maybe twenty feet away. I could see two people, could hear a man's voice saying things but couldn't make out his words.

"Everything all right?" I said.

More choking noises.

A woman said, "Please."

I said, "You okay?"

A man said, "No worry for you," and he whispered something to the woman that I couldn't hear.

She stopped begging.

My maracas shook in ugly seizures.

I looked up and down the street, took a few steps toward the couple, tossed my cigarette down, and heard the harsh sound of weight being thrown against a corrugated garage door, the man's silhouette slamming the woman into the clamoring metal, two times, three times, four. He pulled his hand back and slapped her and she fell to the sidewalk, and the man, still standing, his legs splayed to straddle her face, leaned over and choked her again. He picked her head up and shook it, hit it on the concrete.

"Stop!" I said.

I ran at him. He kept choking her. I kept running and he kept choking, and I was there. I was with them. I was with her. And this was when the world forfeited its volume, the three of us engulfed in a gaping quiet. We were there. Breathing. Tussling. We manufactured our normal human noises, but I couldn't hear any of them because I was helping her.

I punched him in the cheek and he fell down, springing back up and running away.

"You all right?" I said, and she blinked her eyes slower than I'd ever seen anyone blink, so slow, like she'd just woken from a coma after decades of devastating sleep. Her creaking atrophied eyelids bouncing, adjusting to the new light, this new world. She kept blinking, and I told her to go to Damascus and have them call the cops. She nodded, another new movement, testing the neck after all those years frozen. "Do you know what to do?" I said and another nod from her, and I said, "You're safe," and bolted after him, having no idea what I'd do if I caught up, and even with a pack-a-day habit, I ran fast, Olympic fast. Soon I gained on him, feeling my adrenaline, the venom that lets mothers lift cars off their children's legs, rollicking in me. I could feel it hurtle through my veins, demanding revenge, demanding that this man pay for what he'd done. He couldn't treat her like this; people couldn't treat others any awful way they wanted to. I'd made sure Letch learned that lesson, and I'd teach this guy the same thing. He was only a step ahead of me so I jumped on him, wrapped my arms around his waist, pulling him down, both of us crashing into the sidewalk, in a flailing heap.

I grabbed his hair. Cocked my arm back. Ready to smash one of my microwave popcorn bags into his face. But before I brought my fist to his mouth, he hit me. Hard. He was a southpaw, and what must have been his wedding ring cut into my nose. It had some kind of gem jetting up from the band because something sharp, like a nail, punctured my skin. My nose leaking blood. I brought my hands up to cover my face. He hit me again. I dropped to the ground. He kicked me. In the ribs and the face. Six times. He left me there.

———

Me, Rhonda, limping back to the bar. I fished a crumpled newspaper from the gutter to wipe at my nose, smeared blood all over the front page, all over a picture of President Bush, another baffled expression spattered across his face. I balled it up and threw it in the gutter, next to a tipped over construction cone. I staggered past a homeless man pushing a shopping cart full of plastic orange jack-o-lanterns; he had a sign hanging from the front of the cart that said *Donate to the United Negro Pizza Fund.*

When I walked back into Damascus, the bar erupted with applause. Everyone held their drinks up in my direction.

"The man of the hour!" my friend, the bartender, said.

The hooker, her name was Karla, sat at the bar, patting the stool next to her. She must have been about forty. She wore so much makeup that it looked like she'd rubbed refried beans on her cheeks. She seemed pretty collected considering what she'd just been through. My mom was always pretty collected afterward, too. A welt rose under Karla's left eye. A small gash on her forehead. No amount of refried beans would conceal these things.

"My hero," she said. "Let me buy you a drink."

She wasn't blinking like she'd come out of a coma any longer. "Did you call the cops?"

"We don't need the cops."

"We need the cops."

"Forget it. Let's have a drink."

I sat down, and she examined my face. Under a streetlight, I'd already measured the damage in a car's side mirror: I knew about the cut on my nose, the skin peeled off my cheek and chin, the purple halo of bruise around my eye. The weird thing was that Karla seemed more concerned about my injuries than her own. She traced my bruise-halo with her fingertip and said, "Poor baby."

"It's not so bad," I said, which wasn't true. The guy had really done a number on me, but right then, nothing hurt. People admired me. My wounds gleamed like trophies.

Vern stormed over and handed me a warm one, which it looked like he'd already had a few sips from. "Good work, soldier," he said and before I answered, he stomped back to his barstool.

Karla rolled her eyes, shook her head, finally reaching over and cupping my face in her hands. "How about a freebie?"

"Sex?"

"Why not?"

"No thanks."

She looked baffled that I'd insult her generosity. "I'll take care of everything, baby. I'm a trained professional." She kissed me. And because of the way her lips felt on my aching face, I'd have done anything she said.

Every person in the bar, maybe thirteen people total, wanted to buy me a drink, and who was I to say no? I'd never felt the UV rays of the limelight before, never known that kind of tepid fame. It was marvelous, our collective race to oblivion. We drank whiskey as if the world wouldn't make it to tomorrow's traffic jams. We listened to rock and roll on the jukebox. We sang along. Karla kissed me in the most astonishing ways, using her tongue on my Adam's apple, and even though I hadn't showered in days, she licked the briny film of alcoholic sweat from my skin. A little after one a.m. she said, "Let's have sex," and we loped out of Damascus, arm in arm.

It was a warm night, September in San Francisco, Indian summer. You could actually see the stars. Not that many, but it was better than nothing.

————

Karla asked if I'd like to take a shower while she changed her sheets. I took it as a hint and agreed. My head spun as I stood in the stream, washing my body, my hair, using her toothbrush, which I'd found tucked behind the bar soap. I was even going to shave, but she said, "I'd like to clean your wounds," through the steam.

I hadn't heard Karla come in the bathroom, couldn't really see her. I looked down, and my cock had shriveled to a clump, barely visible through the mangy fur. "I'm not sure I can do this," I said.

"Don't worry. I've taken miles of dick."

"Maybe we can just sleep?"

"Why?"

"I'm not feeling very... able."

"There's no reason to be intimidated," she said. "Just aim for the walls."

"But I – "

"I've got a reputation to protect."

"But – "

"Sshh," she said, telling me to get out of the shower. When I opened the curtain, she stood there holding an open towel, like a mother. She dried me off. The towel felt amazing as it snaked around my body. Karla started with my legs and worked her way up. "Turn around," she said, and rubbed the towel across my back and arms, reaching around to my face, finally fitting the towel on my head, turban-style. Its extra heft made it hard to keep my head straight.

Karla soaked cotton balls in hydrogen peroxide and ran them over the shiners on my face and arms. I smiled.

"Does that feel good?" she asked.

"Better than anything."

I smiled again. Her hands felt wonderful mopping my face with the cotton balls. So relaxed, my head lolled and the turban unraveled and fell off.

———

Twenty minutes later we walked into her bedroom. She took off her clothes; Karla had a tattoo running down the middle of her back. She said it was a Mayan column, stacked stones, drawn all in black. "I retrofitted my spine," she said, told me she had no choice but to reinforce it after all the crap her ex-husband had put her through.

"What happened?"

"Bad enough he treated me that way in the first place. I'm not going to keep it alive by thinking about it anymore." She hit the light and climbed in bed, kissing me on the cheek.

I can tell you that being in bed with her was magnificent, that it made every kick and punch from that man worth it. I felt nauseated and my face ached and my ribs were killing me, but I was happy. Do you understand that? I fell into a hibernating sleep, curled in her armpit, my nose almost touching her nipple, curled into her warmth, and it was so perfect, just that perfect, her fingers scratching the nape of my neck. You could have thrown us in a coffin and covered us with dirt. It wouldn't have mattered to me.

LOVE YOURSELF, RHONDA

Letch taught me how to make Bloody Marias from scratch. Tequila, Tabasco, tomato juice, lemon juice, Worcestershire, horseradish, salt, and pepper.

"Put your balls into it," Letch said. That phrase was the only piece of fathering he ever gave me except this: he'd been teaching me to love myself. The first time he mentioned it, he made a masturbatory gesture in front of his crotch, up and down, ferociously slow.

"How do I love myself?" I said.

"Do it fast," he said.

————

Letch was mom's latest boyfriend and he called me Rhonda because he said that was a dumb blonde name and that I was a dumb blonde, as in, "Are you queer, Rhonda?" and "Make me another Bloody Maria, Rhonda." I was a boy so I didn't like being called a girl's name, and my hair was black, but Letch was a tough guy so I had to let the whole Rhonda thing slide.

I walked to the kitchen and Letch was eating a bowl of Lucky Charms, complaining about the way the house looked. "We're not animals," he said. "Can't you keep this place clean?"

"Sorry," I said, wondering when mom would come home this time. She'd been going on her disappearing acts more and more, taking off for a few days at a time, leaving me money to order pizzas. The worst was how she'd act once she got home, all annoyed as I followed her around the house.

"I know it's hard without your ma around, but she'll be back soon," he said. "Until then, you're responsible for cleaning up around here. Make me a drink."

Letch went back to his Lucky Charms, pushing gigantic spoonfuls of *yellow diamonds, purple horseshoes* into his big mouth. "That's a faggot's haircut, Rhonda," he said.

————

There wasn't anyone in the barbershop except a pretty blonde woman wearing white jeans. Her hair was styled high, all space-age. She didn't look that much older than me.

The shop didn't have any air conditioning, and it was way over one-hundred degrees outside. July in Arizona.

"This boy needs a grooming," Letch said to her, holding a Bloody Maria. "Can you clean up his mess?"

He walked away without waiting for an answer. He lay down on a bench scattered with magazines, set his cocktail on the floor, and shut his eyes. "I'm sweating like a faggot eating a corndog!" he said, bellyaching, but it didn't seem like he was talking to either of us. Letch sent a clumsy hand searching for his Bloody Maria, sucked a few ice cubes into his mouth and chewed.

She laughed a little, looked at me in a way I thought her stomach might hurt. "Come on, cowboy," she said, and I climbed into a gray chair, under a gray smock. She sprayed my hair with water and combed it straight back, curls wet enough to fall down flat. "Do you know what you want?"

"I want to fix myself," I said.

She giggled.

Inches of black curls flew around my face, landing on my stomach, falling to the floor. There wasn't any music playing, and the smack of the scissors sounded loud in my ears. Letch slept on the bench.

I noticed a small picture of her and a boy, probably her son, taped to the mirror's lower corner. They were in front of a

Christmas tree, lying on their stomachs, wearing matching red sweaters. The boy looked about two years old.

"Is that your son?"

"That's my Michael."

"Do you love him?"

"Of course I love him," she said. "He's my son."

I hated her son. Hated Michael. Hated her love and really hated those Christmas sweaters. Under the smock, I rubbed it through my pants. Squeezed it, pinched the tip to wake it up, and I started to get hard, cupping my hand around its shape. I undid my fly and pulled it out and loved myself. I bent it to the side a little, sending a shiver down my spine. I tried to keep my facial expressions consistent, a fixed frown so she wouldn't notice what I was doing.

"I'm loving myself," I said, forcing a pitiful smile as I looked at her in the mirror.

She didn't know what was going on under the surface.

"It really does look good," she said and took a step back and admired her work.

My arm bounced under the smock. Was I crying?

She stopped cutting my hair. All my pretty curls were gone. She'd given me one of those marine haircuts, high and tight. Before I could say anything else, Letch woke up and walked over to us. "No more homo-hair for Rhonda. She put her balls into that cut, hey?" He fuzzed my head with his hand.

I looked at her in the mirror. "Of course you love him," I said. "He's your son."

My tiny balls ached. I needed to finish loving myself so I went to the bathroom. I had to get hard again so I thought about the stylist, imagined her wearing only that Christmas sweater, spreading her legs and telling me *I love you*, and she invited me to climb on top of her, and for just a second, the fantasy felt real enough that I thought I could open my eyes and I'd see her there, underneath me, the two of us loving each other. I threw my eyelids open but all I saw was me, my reflection blasted back in my face by that awful mirror – there I was, standing in the bathroom with my pants at my ankles. It was humiliating so I closed my eyes again and hoped to find that image of her lying with her legs spread wide, but she was gone, and I saw nothing so I yelled, "Of course you love him, of course you love him, of course you love him," and I felt the pressure building, and she and Letch must have heard me screaming because they were at the door, Letch demanding that I open up, but he wasn't going to take this moment away from me, he couldn't break down the door and I felt safe so I kept yelling, "Of course you love him, of course you love him, of course you love your own son!" and I could hear his fists thrashing the door, the woman asking him to stop, to calm down – *I don't think this is helping* – and then she talked to me, asked if she could come in, if I'd please let her in, but that just made me scream louder, "Of course you love your own son!" and part of me was hoping my mom would show up, that she was ready to stop disappearing all the time, and I was almost ready to let loose, it was building and building, felt like something wonderful was about to happen, so I yelled it one last time, "Of course you love your own son!" but there wasn't a climax, no fantastic orgasm, just a few measly drops, and it hurt more than it felt good. I left the pathetic dribbles on the floor, under the sink, in a lumpy pattern like the horseradish I used in Letch's Bloody Marias.

I wanted her to find my mess. I wanted her and Michael to wipe the floor together. It could be a family activity. Maybe they could use their Christmas sweaters to sop it up. Yuletide fun.

I washed my hands. Splashed water on my face and sat down on the floor. Letch kept pounding, but I wasn't going to come out for a while.

FAUCET OF EMBARRASSMENT

Karla and I, our drunken bodies flopped around her bed. We'd tangled in such a way that my arm was trapped underneath her back. It fell asleep. I could feel my pulse stomping out its rhythm in my trapped limb. I counted every pop of blood. Seven. Nine. I counted as I lay there, worrying about my circulation. Worrying because my hands were always losing their feeling. Going dead on me. But I didn't want to move, didn't want to ruin the way that Karla wanted to be in bed with me. Seventeen. I couldn't ruin this night with Karla, even as she smothered the life from my arm.

Almost as soon as she'd turned out the lights, Karla had given in to the fatigue of whiskey. She snored, churned. Her body rummaged under the covers, restless in a way that made me think she was having nightmares.

Was I in it? Was I it?

I couldn't fall asleep because I had such a dire case of the bed spins: the ceiling raced before my eyes in tight orbits, the ceiling bending clockwise and coming around again. Blacks and grays smeared across my open eyes; I couldn't close them or the spinning would torque to mean speeds. I felt weightless, watching the colors curve and drop like shooting stars.

Twenty-one. Twenty-four.

Still I couldn't sleep, lying with Karla. A woman who wanted me to be here.

Not just my maraca, but my whole arm numbing now, drifting away.

This had happened to my feet, too, the freeze creeping its way through them. Thirty. It was always happening, this feeling like my own limbs were leaving me and floating off. Karla wanted to have a freebie and maybe I should have tried. Thirty-six. Bursts of blood jumping in my vein, in that spot between my bicep and forearm. Every time it blasted, it was louder, sounding like grenades in my ears, and they drowned out my thoughts. Forty-one. I couldn't hear what I was thinking. All those thoughts, the thoughts I must have been having. I must have been thinking about Karla, about kissing her mouth and saying that I'd like to let her try. There was no way that I could have been thinking about anything else. Fifty-nine. Just the pulse. The noise of popping blood blaring louder than grenades. I couldn't stand it, couldn't let this go on a second longer because my eardrums might explode, the membranes ripping and launching and splattering like phlegm in a sneeze.

Seventy.

I needed to get her off of my arm, but I didn't want to move, didn't want to ruin this, and then I noticed I was pissing. Right in her bed. It soaked my legs, wormed its way up the small of my back. How long had I been going? No way to know. So many warm ones and whiskey shots, it could have been an hour. Eighty-three. With my free hand, I felt around, and yeah, the whole middle of the bed was drenched, and I kept thinking, stop wrecking this, don't spoil it. I needed to get my arm out from under Karla, but if I moved her, she'd notice the condition of the bed and I didn't want that to happen. All I could do was lie there, helpless, waiting for my eardrums to rupture. All I could do was wait for my arm to buzz itself for so long that it couldn't ever wake up, limp and useless.

———

The next thing I knew Karla shook and hit me. "Wake up," she said. "How could you do this?"

Me, Rhonda, trying to steady my clogged head, an ocean of liquor sloshing from ear to ear.

I said, "What?" and she said, "Get out of here," and I said, "Why?" and she grabbed my hand and shoved it in between my legs. Into that damp faucet of embarrassment. "Get out of here," she said, standing up. "I bring you to my house, and this is the thanks I get?!"

I fell out of her bed.

She searched for my clothes and threw them at me. "You're pathetic," she said and launched a shoe, which hit me in the face. "I'm so stupid for bringing you here."

I tried to get dressed as fast as I could, but I was still drunk and falling over, not understanding why she was so mad. I put on my clothes but couldn't find my jacket so I ran out of the room without it and she yelled after me, "Only babies wet the bed."

"I'm sorry," I said. "I'll clean it up."

"Just get out!"

I tried to calm her down, promised I'd clean everything up, but she wasn't listening, kept saying that I'd wet the bed like a pathetic little baby, that she couldn't believe someone who'd been so brave a few hours ago had pissed her sheets.

She kept yelling, and the more she yelled, the madder I got.

"I could have let him kill you," I said.

"Only little babies wet the bed."

I didn't want to hear her talk like that so I stumbled down the hallway, trying to block out the attack of her words, but it was like the whole world had halted and quieted to eavesdrop.

"Does the baby need to go potty?" she said.

The whole world, an army of ears pressed to the walls. Prying open windows. Reading Karla's lips.

"Would you like to sit on the potty, baby?"

I opened her front door.

"Big boys sit on the potty," she said. "Are you a big boy?"

I said, "I saved your life."

I said, "You're welcome," and ran out of her apartment.

TELL ME

There will be ten of them, he said. Tell me what you see, he
said. Flashcards flashing, symmetrical patterns splattered across
them. His office smelled like tuna fish, and his wrists were
thin. I always thought they were probably brittle like uncooked
angel-hair pasta. Usually he sat in front of me, but this time
he was next to me. Usually we'd be face to face, and his eyes
would pop back and forth, first on my left eye, then on my right
eye, then on my left eye. His eyes popping. Tell me, he said. He
held a stack of cardboard cards. He told me to relax. He told
me there wasn't anything to worry about. I wasn't worried until
he said that. There were diplomas all over the wall behind him,
one window in the middle of them, a metal grating across the
window. Right eye. He handed me the first flashcard. Black ink
on a white background. He was sitting next to me. We were
alone. It was my turn to be with him, and none of the kids
liked being in his office. He had a severe limp, almost tipping
over as he walked, and we made up stories about it. Mine was,
Landmine in Korea. Another kid said, Diabetic so they hacked
it off. Just tell me what you see, he said, but I never saw simple
things. Never could say that I saw a woman's chest or a mime
or a monster. I saw stories. I saw memories. Left eye. I called
him Dr. Angel-Hair because his wrists were so thin and fragile.
He'd shift in his chair when I didn't answer right away. I'd stare
at the pictures. Zone out. Remember. Betray. Love. Tell me, he
said, and I told a story about Letch. Told him that Letch made

me a grilled cheese sandwich with string cheese on April Fools Day, that we laughed, that we hugged, that I made him a Bloody Maria. I told him that Letch covered the walls of my room with posters of girls in bikinis because he wasn't going to raise no faggot. New flashcard. Black and red ink. This one was my mom. Just her face. From her eyebrows to her chin. Can I have that one, I said, and he said, Why, and I said, Forget it. Diplomas decorated the wall behind him. After Letch had put the girls up in my room, he asked me if I liked them and he told me to pretend that they were my harem. I said, What's a harem, and he said, What are they teaching you in school. My mom, her face was like mine, from the eyebrows to the chin, freckles and green eyes, too pale to live in the desert. Too exposed. Not cut out for those conditions. Sunburns. Another card with black and red ink. When we first moved there, my mom would rub aloe vera on my sunburns, on the days I'd scorched my skin the color of cooked ham. One-hundred-eighteen degrees in the summer. Flashcard flashing. Black ink. Tell me. Can I turn this one upside down, I said, and he said, Whatever you'd like. It was Letch again, asking if I'd like to see what a woman can do. If I'd like to see some hardcore action. I would, I said. Letch came back, armed with a cache of dirty movies. You like blowjobs, he said. What's blowjobs, I said. Tell me, the doctor said. Tell me what you see, he said. Usually his eyes popped back and forth. There was always the smell of tuna fish in his office. Metal grating on the window. Another kid thought the doctor's leg was intact but that he had a bum knee, an old football injury. Blowjobs are when a girl puts your cock in her mouth, he said. Right eye. Next card, black again, and this one was something from the hospital. It was the pattern on the tile. I always stared at it while I showered. Diamonds connected. Beautiful black diamonds outlined on a white background. I liked to watch TV, but they never let me watch horror movies. Do a puzzle, they said. Read. Play cards. Mom let me watch whatever movies I wanted. She'd leave and I'd watch movies and sometimes Letch and I watched movies about blowjobs. Look at her go, he said. Left eye then on my right eye then on my left eye. Next card: black ink: our old house, the one that moved. Rooms like rafts drifting away from one another. I kept staring and the house came to life, we were all in there, the three of us, me hiding, mom drinking, Letch waiting. Blowjobs are when a girl puts your cock in her mouth, he said. Have you ever had a cock in your mouth, he said. Tell me what you see. Tell me. The next splattered pattern: black ink. Angel-Hair took notes. The story of the grilled cheese on April Fools Day had a happy ending because Letch said, I owe you one, and he ordered a pizza, any toppings I wanted. Extra cheese, I said, and we both laughed. The seventh card, again the ink was all black. They'd fight. Letch and mom. Shouting. He hated how she'd leave all the lights on. Are you in the kitchen, he'd say. Well are you in the kitchen or not. How can you be in two places at once. This is what he'd say while she was in the bathroom and even if he hit her, she never turned the lights off, only on, only turning the lights on, never off. Right eye. He hated how the whole world was rigged, fixed. He fixed engines. He picked little black smiles out from under his fingernails with a steak knife. Another kid thought the doctor had a clubfoot. Next card. Gorgeous colors. Pink and blue and gray and orange. My dad, where was he, somewhere, where, somewhere. Why couldn't I go with him. He had new kids that needed his attention, my mom said. Blowjobs ended with a mouthful of salty chutney. Another explosion of color, green and orange and pink, and the bikini-girls in my room all smiled. They were in paradise. Palm trees. Under waterfalls. On pale beaches. One was on the hood of a Ferrari. She didn't smile but pursed her lips. You could see the dark hue and shape of her nipples through the white bikini. Flashcard flashed and it was pink and blue and gray and green and yellow and orange, and Tell me what you see, he said, and there was the night my mom got another DUI. I was in the car with her. Letch wasn't there. She kept laughing. She kept saying to the cop, I can't believe this. She kept saying, Don't you guys have anything better to do. The cop told her to take off her high heels and walk a straight line, heel to toe, heel to toe, and she took two steps and ran her hose and slapped him and she was bawling by the time we got to the police station. I spent the night there, watching "M*A*S*H" reruns with a cop, waiting for Letch to come and get me. I was starving and the cop gave me a glass of orange juice and a peanut butter cookie. The doctor's wrists were thin and brittle like angel-hair pasta and when he stared at me his eyes popped back and forth, always popping. Letch rolled the black smiles from underneath his fingernails into little globes and flicked them across the room. Left eye. Right eye. Tell me. Tell me everything you see.

KEEP DIGGING

After I left Karla's house, I stood at a bus stop, shivering in a T-shirt. I'd left my jacket in her apartment. The fog had reached the outer Mission district and I didn't have enough money for a cab and couldn't walk the twenty blocks to my apartment, not after the beating that guy had given me.

I stood there, covered in piss. Clammy humiliation fastened all over me. Stood there, making fists, my maracas so cold, tingly. I blew into them, almost hyperventilating, trying to heat them up, but my breath smelled acrid as it ricocheted off of my palms and slipped up my nose. Stood there trying to understand why Karla would do that to me. Trying to fathom how you treat a hero like filth. How you mock the man who saved your life, calling him *pathetic little baby*. How you make your hero feel so tiny that you'd need a microscope to know he was there.

Me, Rhonda, standing at the bus stop, shuddering and making fists, trying to understand what had happened, why it had happened, but the longer I stood on the empty street, no cars going by except an occasional taxi that I couldn't afford, things in my head mutated, whirled, and then it wasn't Karla's fault. No, there was nothing wrong with her; she hadn't done a thing. It was me, making all the wrong choices. It was my fault. I'd taken a night that could have been perfect and dismantled it. It was like what I'd done in Phoenix, and right when I thought about that place, that time, my mom, Letch, the antifreeze, that was when I saw the kid.

I didn't know it was a kid, at first, only a shadow, facing me. I could feel it staring, standing directly across the street. The shadow flashed a light, off and on, off and on. And then he called to me, "Do you know Morse code?" It flashed, off and on, different intervals between the light and dark.

"Me?" I said, squinting.

"This is an S-O-S!"

"What is?"

The boy walked across the street, toward me. The light still flashing. Coming from the boy's arms. As he got closer, I could see that he held a miner's helmet.

I shielded my eyes. "Do you mind?"

"Do you like magic?" He put the helmet on his head, its light left on.

He looked familiar, eleven, maybe twelve years old.

"Can you magically make the bus come?" I said.

"Would you like to see a trick?"

"Go ahead."

"Not here."

"Do I know you?"

He laughed, flipping his helmet's light off. "Do you know me?" He laughed harder. "That's a good one."

The feeling in my hands changed. They weren't buzzing anymore. No. Now they felt like apples. Apples with worms slinking through their tainted meat.

He flipped the light back on. Blinding. I put my hands up, trying to block it out. I said, "You're hurting my eyes," and he said, "Aren't you used to getting hurt?" and I got a pounding headache. Things I didn't think about. Things I never let myself think about traveled over old and rusted wires. Flashes of old footage. Static and flickers and frames. Images of this boy. All the stuff that Dr. Angel-Hair told me wasn't real: the way our house's rooms had drifted away from one another, the sidewinders who loved me.

"Who are you?" I said, my shivers getting worse, my worm-riddled hands still held up to try and shield my eyes from his helmet's vicious beam.

"I'm Rhonda," he said. "I'm you."

———

This was later. Maybe an hour. After we'd walked back to my apartment, my hand on the kid's shoulder, using him like a human crutch. After we walked down 24th Street toward Valencia, past a group of young Latinos standing in front of a taqueria, El Farolito, listening to hip-hop. After we turned onto Valencia Street and saw the hulking shapes of dormant construction equipment parked on the side of the road, those monsters of renovation. After we stepped on a message that someone had stenciled on the sidewalk in purple spray paint: *An eye for an eye and the world goes blind*. After the wind pushed an open umbrella by us, which was weird because it hadn't rained in six or seven months. After little-Rhonda helped me up the stairs of my building. After I put a jacket on, and after he watched me drink a couple of beers.

"We have to go," little-Rhonda said. The light on his helmet was still on, but besides that, he looked like a typical kid: jeans, sneakers, a T-shirt. Dark hair and green eyes.

"This isn't real," I said. "Like the sidewinders."

"These sidewinders?" he said, jamming his hand in his pocket and coming out with two of them. They slithered up his arm, each coiling on one of his shoulders and purring.

"They're real?"

"Of course, they're real."

I stuck my face up to one of the snakes, its tongue flitting against my cheek. "What are you doing here?" I asked little-Rhonda.

"I'm your escort."

"To where?"

The snakes moved back down his arm and into his pocket: "You're going to love this."

―――――

I lived on the corner of 20th and Valencia, above a used bookstore. About five a.m. little-Rhonda and I walked to a dumpster a few blocks away. The streets were almost deserted, except for some homeless people leaning against a French restaurant, smoking. One of the guys had his shopping cart tied to his thigh with an extension cord, so no one could steal it once he fell asleep. He asked little-Rhonda and me if we had any vodka to donate to charity.

"What charity?" I said.

"This one," he said and opened his mouth, pointing down his throat.

The fog had gone, a crescent moon visible, which was yellow and lay on its side looking like a jaundiced smile.

When we got to the dumpster, little-Rhonda told me to climb inside of it.

"Why?"

"Trust me," he said.

"Why?"

"Because I'm the only person who hasn't hurt you."

I heard a rattle come from little-Rhonda's pocket, some purring-assurance from an old friend.

The dumpster was stashed behind another taqueria. It must have dumped the leftover food that couldn't be saved, because the dumpster was totally full. There were pinto and black beans, chicken, prawns, beef, guacamole, smashed chips. In one corner, what looked like tortilla soup dribbled through the trash; at least, I hoped it was tortilla soup.

"Get in," he said.

"For what?"

"At the bottom, there's a trapdoor."

I stood on top of the trash, trying to kick some to the sides, to burrow lower without having to get my hands dirty, but it wasn't working. I tried to tell myself that this made sense. That it made sense because I was doing this for me. For little-Rhonda. If anyone else had asked, I would have said no. But this was different. Plus he had the sidewinders, and the snakes always loved me and they wouldn't let anything bad happen so I dropped to my knees, right there in the dumpster, dropped to them and used my hands to scoop all that food and trash out of the way, but it was like trying to dig a hole in sand, in the desert, grains sliding back into the space I'd just cleared. I looked at little-Rhonda and said, "Why don't you help me?" and he said, "I am," and I said, "No, why don't you get in here and help me?" and he said, "Keep digging." I threw the trash out, onto the sidewalk, really digging deep. I shoveled all that wasted food, and when I finally reached the bottom, little-Rhonda was right: there was a trapdoor. I opened it. I saw a ladder but couldn't see how far down it went.

"I found it," I said, but he didn't answer me. I stood up, looked all around, but he was gone.

ANTIFREEZE

Our house first broke, its rooms drifting away from one another like the separating continents, on the day my mom said she didn't believe me. "He wouldn't do that," she said. "He loves you."

"Loves me? He's only lived with us for a week."

This was in Phoenix, Arizona. In the early 1980s.

"Don't ruin this for me," my mom said, telling me to get her another pain pill. Then she told me she couldn't thaw any dinner because her arthritis was killing her, that she'd tried to play her Casio keyboard and now she suffered the consequences. She said sometimes her hands hurt so bad they felt like she had poison oak under the skin. She'd had rheumatoid since I was born. In her wrists, her jaw, her knees. She was always taking pills to murder the throbbing in her joints. She was always washing the pills down with box wine. Chablis. She pronounced it phonetically, tcha-bliss.

As I shut the door to their room and walked toward the kitchen, there was a noise like the loudest yawn in the world. The house creaked and moaned. The walls shook. At first, I thought we were having an earthquake, but instead of things falling to the ground, the house stretched. I could see the carpet rip in places, desert sand slipping into the house. The window in the hallway cracked down the middle.

"What did you do now?" my mom yelled.

———

People could stand right out front of the house and not see anything unusual, but if they took the time to walk in the front door, they'd have seen that as the rooms dislocated, the hallways stretched to connect them. The desert infiltrated the long halls. Sand continued to wiggle its way through the cracks in the floor and walls. At first, there were only handfuls of sand here and there, but it wasn't long before I couldn't even see the carpet anymore. Each day, too, cacti sprouted, pushing their spiked heads up through the sand, growing a little higher as the months droned on.

During the day, the violent rays of southwestern sunshine blazed in the house's hallways, but at night the temperature fell to freezing. Desert predators – rattle snakes, scorpions, tarantulas, Gila monsters – lived in the house. I learned to coexist with them, to avoid provoking their wraths. Soon I didn't fear the scorpion's stinger or the way a spider's legs felt traipsing on my skin. And the snakes, especially the sidewinders, became my friends: I'd stand still and they'd slither up my leg and coil around my neck or perch on my shoulder. Their tails purred a warning, but the rattle wasn't scary. They'd never bared fangs in my direction.

———

Letch hunted all over the house for me. Late at night. Lumbering through the freezing desert. While my mom was on another disappearing act or after she'd passed out from a relentless suckling of tcha-bliss.

Only six months after the house's first fracturing, there were already miles between the rooms. I'd timed myself, running from their bedroom door to mine. Nine minutes in a full sprint. I timed myself running between my different hiding places. I learned to be invisible.

But one day when I expected him to be at work still, I walked into the kitchen and there he was, watching "The Facts of Life" on TV and cramming full moons of bologna in his mouth.

"Where have you been?" Letch said.

"Have you seen my mom?" I was starving, but I didn't want to stay in the kitchen, in case he was in one of his moods.

He waved a piece of bologna in my face. "Where were you, Rhonda?"

I thought about trying to run, but he was too close, would have caught me in no time and been extra mad for having to hurry. His breath was going to taste terrible.

"We need to talk," he said.

————

I set up a series of small bunkers, holes I'd dug up in the house's sand where I could hide without being seen. Both Letch and my mom had walked right past spots in the sand where I'd concealed myself and they hadn't noticed me.

From these safe places, I tried to talk to my mom. Like a mysterious voice. Like her conscience.

I said, "Why are you always leaving me alone with him?"

I said, "Do you know what he does while you're gone?"

"Stop it!" she said, turning in circles in the hallway, searching for me, but any man-made light was miles away and finding one of my bunkers in the dark was impossible.

"I can tell you every little thing," I said, and she tried to run away, stumbling in the sand, falling over, standing up, staggering away.

————

I hid for so long that my health started to fail. I lost too much weight. Dehydrated and sleeping most of the day, the sidewinders protecting me from him during these long naps.

I knew that my mom wasn't going to save me. All she did was play dumb and defend him and thaw frozen food and drink tcha-bliss. But one freezing night she was on another disappearing act, and Letch went too far with me, and I knew I had to take care of myself.

My best friend's name was Skyler. He and his mom, Madeline, lived a few blocks away. About a week before Letch went too far, I was over at their house, and Madeline complained that she thought their neighbor had poisoned their dog with antifreeze.

"Antifreeze?" I asked, and she told me that all you had to do was mix some antifreeze in with water and once the dog drank it, that was that, no more canine. Skyler and his mom had been fighting about it, because he wanted to get a new dog, but she kept saying what was the point, their neighbor would only do it again and deny the whole thing with an awful smile on his face. And Letch had just gone too far and we were home alone, I don't know where my mom was, don't know where she ever was, and Letch said, "Make me another Bloody Maria," and I limped into the kitchen. The kitchen was next to the garage. There was antifreeze in the garage. Antifreeze could kill a dog if you mixed it with water and the dog drank it. That was that. I made his Bloody Maria. I left a few inches of room at the top of the glass. He hollered at me to hurry up, he was thirsty, god damnit! I opened the garage door. The antifreeze was under Letch's workbench. The workbench used to be right next to the door, but the garage had stretched with the rest of the house. It was dark. It was freezing. I limped through the desert, through the sand. Not many people know how cold the desert is at night. Or how quiet. I struggled to get there and grabbed the antifreeze and made my way back toward the kitchen. I poured it into his Bloody Maria. I poured it in because antifreeze could kill a dog if you mixed it with water and the dog drank it. I stirred it with a spoon, worried he'd be able to taste it, that he wouldn't drink it, and there wouldn't be any *that was that*, and I wouldn't get to look at him like Madeline's and Skyler's neighbor, wouldn't get to deny the whole thing with an awful smile on my face. Letch yelled again for his drink. I stirred it some more. I put in extra Tabasco and pepper to try and hide the taste of the antifreeze.

I made my way through the desert, back to their bedroom, walking past some sidewinders who purred and purred and purred. When I opened the door, Letch said, "Did you put your balls into it?"

I handed him the drink. That was that.

DIVE

I lowered myself through the dumpster's trapdoor and snaked my way down the ladder. It was humid, smelled like tuna fish. There weren't any lights but the farther down I descended, dropping into that galaxy of blackness, the less I was scared. I was used to the infinity of Damascus' all-black paint job.

A voice came from beneath me. "You coming or what?"

I looked down and saw the light coming from little-Rhonda's helmet. Like a hotheaded coach, he clapped his hands and told me to hurry up.

"How'd you get down there?" I said.

"Climb faster."

"What is this place?"

"Come on. Chop, chop."

I made my way down. My arms ached. I should have been counting the ladder's rungs, so I'd know how far I'd dropped, but it was too late now.

"Finally," little-Rhonda said, as my feet hit the floor.

I shook my arms, trying to get the feeling back in them. "Finally," I said back, mimicking him like I was the kid; I used the front of my T-shirt to wipe the sweat from my face.

"Got any smokes?" he said.

"You're a child."

"You smoke."

"I'm older."

"You're me," he said.

I couldn't win.

Little-Rhonda led me through a maze of corridors. He flipped his helmet's light off and asked if I was scared of the dark. "Knock it off," I said. It was so dark that the tip of his cigarette was like a flare, falling in the sky, guiding a rescue ship to someone stranded on an island.

He turned the light back on. "You're no fun."

"Are we in the sewer?"

"No, this is Sweden," he said and threw his cigarette on the ground. "This is a remote cabin in the Andes. This is an ancient Sri Lankan village."

"What are we doing down here?"

We came around another corner, and finally there was some light, a thin sliver of it peeking through the crack at the bottom of a closed door. Little-Rhonda twisted the knob, but before he opened it, he looked back at me and said, "What happens down here is just as important as what happens up there." He pushed the door open.

It was a small empty room. Over near the far wall was a puddle, in the shape of a Rorschach inkblot.

"Do you remember what that is?" he said.

I'd never forget Dr. Angel-Hair. Our talks. Our hours, days, and months, as he pried into me, stretching, trying to make me better. "I remember."

"Touch it."

I leaned over. My finger went into the puddle. The water was cold, oily. "What is it?"

"Jump in it."

"Why?"

"Because."

"Where will I go?"

"And you have to dive into it," he said.

"What?"

"Dive into it."

"Headfirst?"

"Headfirst."

"Why?"

"Trust me."

I didn't answer him.

"Oh, Jesus," he said. "Am I going to have to throw you in?"

Me, Rhonda, scared but knowing I should listen. Like a child learning to dive, I put my hands over my head and stood on the edge of the puddle. I looked at little-Rhonda and he nodded at me. I bent at the waist awkwardly and moved my weight forward and took a huge breath, and my fingers went into the cold oily water, then my arms, my head, my torso, my legs, and I didn't want to open my eyes, knew I probably shouldn't open them since I didn't know what kind of liquid I fell into, but I couldn't stop myself. I opened them but couldn't see a thing, everything black, like freefalling down an elevator shaft filled with espresso. I fell and fell into it, kept wondering if I was going to run out of breath, but I never did. Me, Rhonda, an astronaut slipping farther into the darkness. My body slowed down, still falling but as if attached to an invisible parachute. My feet landed on something solid. I lay down on my stomach and noticed that the bottom of the puddle was made of glass.

Little-Rhonda and my mom were on the other side of the window. He wasn't wearing his miner's helmet, so he looked like I used to look. He sat on the bathroom counter; he had a bloody nose, a swollen cheek. My mom had a bloody nose, too. Seeing them, seeing the way Letch had decorated their faces made me so mad I punched the glass between us, trying to shatter it so I could save them, and even though I was totally submerged, I could talk, yelling, "Hey! Hey!" but they never looked up, didn't know I was there. I could hear them so clearly, talking to each other in whispers.

"We're out of cotton balls, baby," my mom said to him.

"Do we have any toilet paper?"

"No."

"Coffee filters?"

"Sorry."

"Any old fast food napkins?"

She shook her head, saying, "We'll have to use your sock."

She got down onto her knees, removed his shoe, snatched his sock. She tilted it against the hydrogen peroxide bottle and dabbed it against his cheek. He flinched. He said, "Will you sing to me?"

She soaked the sock with more hydrogen peroxide and rubbed it on his cheek's tiny cut. She started singing a John Lennon song; he was her favorite. She only made it through the first few lines before she said, "Do you mind if I hum, baby? My face is killing me."

He nodded and she hummed, her mouth right by his ear. I closed my eyes, and it was like she was by my face: I could feel her breath, could smell the hydrogen peroxide, and having her that close to me was like nothing bad had ever happened.

"Will you clean my nose?" she said to him. He poured some peroxide onto his sock, dabbed away the blood. She pursed her lips. I think she was trying to smile. "Are you hungry, baby?"

He nodded.

"I can thaw some taquitos."

He nodded again, ran the sock under some hot water, scrubbed the last flecks of dried blood off her upper lip. "All done."

"How do I look?" she said.

"Great."

"Aren't you a smooth talker."

"You look really great."

She took the sock from him and leaned down. Where their blood had soaked the sock, it was the pale color a cherry Popsicle stained its stick. She slipped it back on his foot, the shoe after. "Do you want to help me with the taquitos?"

He nodded again; she kissed him; they walked out of the bathroom.

I tried to follow them but knocked into the wall. The space I was in was no wider than the backseat of a taxi. I sat down again, hoping they'd come back to the bathroom. If I waited long enough, they'd have to, because Letch would give them new shiners to clean.

I would have waited forever, just to hear her hum again, but I was running out of breath.

SOME THINGS THAT MEANT THE WORLD TO ME

Next thing I knew a Mexican man shoved his finger in my face. *"Capitán Basura!"* he shouted, poking me hard in the cheek. Then he changed the timbre of his voice to imitate an emasculated Caucasian: "Check out time, sir. How was your stay? Did you enjoy any treats from the mini-bar?" He hit his palm on the side of the dumpster, howling, yelling to one of his coworkers, in English, to come outside, you won't believe it, take a look at this fucking guy.

I didn't say anything but tried to get my footing on that topsy-turvy heap of trash. I could barely stand up straight, put my arms out like a tightrope walker. "Will you help me get out?" I pleaded.

"Get lost," he said to me and switched to Spanish, saying something to his friend who had just walked up. They did a complicated handshake – palms slapping and twisting, fingers snapping. His friend said to him, "He doesn't look homeless."

"I'm not," I said, climbing out, walking away, scratching my head. Something wet clumped in my hair. I didn't remember falling asleep in the dumpster. I wrung my memory, but there wasn't anything besides blackness, and sometimes things were so black they were more than a color: they were a place, a lonely solar system.

I walked onto Valencia. It was early, maybe eight a.m. The fog slithered down Twin Peaks into the Mission. Pretty soon the air would be wet and carrying the faintest taste of the ocean. Scrawny trees lined the street, and they were losing their leaves, tiny brown bodies falling to the pavement like dying butterflies.

I stepped on another stenciled message on the sidewalk, this one in red paint. It had an arrow pointing toward new luxury condos and said: *Let's gentrify like it's going out of style!*

I approached 19th Street and noticed the construction zone. The yellow machines ready to rip into the asphalt. The tired men in orange vests and hard hats, sipping from coffee cups. San Francisco had been replacing the water mains under Valencia Street for months now. One of the workers fired up a jackhammer. Too much scraping chaos for my hangover, so I turned toward Bartlett Alley. Caffeine was my chief priority, followed by a shower to scrub the dumpster from my body, the moist clump from my hair. But as I took the turn onto Bartlett, about thirty feet away from the coffee shop, there was a homeless guy sleeping on the sidewalk with a splayed pizza box covering his face.

I took him as a sign. A symbol sent from the universe, a reminder that things could be worse. I looked around, but I swear that suddenly the streets were lifeless, abandoned, and when did that happen, the streets of the Mission district vacant, no pedestrians or cars or buses or bike riders? Even the clouds were fixed in the sky. Just me and the homeless man in our suspended moment. I looked down at him: his face curled inside a cardboard box that must have smelled like cheese and processed meat and had a snow angel of grease leached onto its piece of wax paper. Things could be worse. I mean, I could be sleeping on the street and using a pizza box as a pair of sunglasses.

I stood, staring at him. Feeling newly optimistic. Yes, I'd woken up in a dumpster, but I had an apartment to go to and I'd get another job soon, and I needed to stop being so hard on myself. I needed to make sure and remember this guy and his pizza box because even when things didn't seem like they could get any worse, there were always grotesque mutations.

I studied his filthy clothes, jeans and black T-shirt. We were wearing the exact same thing, and I wondered: what if this feeling faded away? What if I woke up tomorrow still stunned by the sleeping man, but the next day, the memory grew stale, and in a couple weeks I barely remembered seeing his agony, and next year it was as if I'd never witnessed him at all?

So I took off running to Walgreens, on the corner of 23rd and Mission, to buy a disposable camera. I wasn't going to let a gift like this disappear and I walked into the store and a muzak version of a John Lennon song that my mom used to sing played, its timeless melody reduced to the barbiturate of background noise.

I combed Walgreens' aisles looking for the cameras, walked by products to pluck and bleach and conceal and color. So many shades of brown to dye your hair. Chestnut, almond, cocoa, caramel. I walked by curling irons and greeting cards and ear drops. Finally, I had to ask an employee where the cameras were and she said that they were behind the counter and I paid for one and ran back to where the man had been sleeping. He was right where I'd left him, sprawled on the sidewalk in front of a used furniture store, its exterior painted like an Irish flag.

The streets were still empty. Miraculously empty. Their bustle erased. Not a peep from any jackhammers. I took the camera out of its cardboard box and wound it and snapped a bunch of photos, probably ten. I didn't want to bother the guy, just needed a few decent pictures of my milestone.

I tiptoed away from the sleeping man. Part of me wanted to thank him, but he had no idea he was my miracle.

———

As I walked toward the café, carrying my disposable camera, my indispensable pictures, all the hibernating animals of the neighborhood revived themselves. Cars and buses whizzed down the streets. Construction machines like prehistoric carnivores carved into the meat of the road. Passersby clad for downtown jobs power-walked to the BART station. A homeless woman had a dead houseplant in her shopping cart, her arms so skinny they looked like prosciutto wrapped around pigeon bones.

"Home is where the heart is," she said, holding the withered houseplant out to me.

———

One more stop on my way back to the apartment, after leaving the café. I needed some cigarettes, a cherry on top of any strong cup of black coffee.

Since it was so early, though, all the liquor stores weren't open yet, and I had to go up to the one on Dolores and 22nd Street. Stepped on another sidewalk stenciling that said, *Stop the war for oil. Ride a bike.*

I walked in, and there was a young woman standing behind the counter. What can I tell you about the way she looked that won't reduce her to pounds, feet, inches? Hair and eye color? The hollow information from a driver's license. I can tell you she had a sexy belly jetting out from under her shirt, a haze of dark hairs around her bellybutton. When I went to sleep that night, I pretended my pillow was her stomach.

"Pack of Camels," I said.

For a few seconds, she didn't move to get the cigarettes, standing back there and looking at me as if the carcasses of my failures were mounted all over my face like taxidermy. Mercifully, she turned around to grab them, and I surveyed the other merchandise behind the counter – booze and condoms mostly, but also a felt outline of a country that said "Jordan" underneath it. One of the boxes of condoms said "Magnum, extra-large."

When she tossed the cigarettes on the counter, I said, "I'll take some Magnums, too," because sometimes you need people to think there's something out of the ordinary about you.

The Jordanian Girl looked at me. Smirked. Blushed. Said, "You a big boy, huh?"

I laughed. "Yeah, I'm a big boy."

She put the cigarettes and condoms in a plastic bag. It didn't seem like she'd noticed the dumpster's smell all over me, the homeless cologne. "I moved in down the street so you'll be seeing lots of me," I said, not wanting to lie to her but needing a reason to start coming here as often as I could.

"What were you taking pictures of?" the Jordanian Girl said and pointed at my camera. Again, I didn't want to lie, but I worried that the truth might make her look at me the same way she had when I'd first entered the store, like I was a failure, and I couldn't bear that. "I take pictures of the neighborhood."

"Buildings? People? All the construction?"

"Pigeons."

She grimaced. "They're so ugly."

"That's what I like about them."

"Their ugliness?"

"The fact that they can't hide it," I said. "The rest of us spend our whole lives trying to trick each other."

"Are you tricking me?"

I picked up the bag with the condoms, felt a gust of embarrassment. "Can I take your picture?"

She shook her head. "This pigeon doesn't like to have her picture taken."

"Maybe next time."

"Anything is possible, but I wouldn't hold my breath."

I breathed as much air into my lungs as I could, cheeks ballooning out. About ten seconds later I exhaled, red-cheeked, dizzy, ready to pass out.

"You should quit smoking," she said.

HOME-COOKED MEAL #1

One time I told my mom and Letch that I wanted to cook dinner for them.

"No way," Letch said. "Cooking skills are hereditary."

My mom laughed, almost spit some tcha-bliss out of her mouth. Everyone knew she could barely thaw dinner, let alone cook anything. "Don't listen to him, baby. We'd love for you to cook us dinner."

"Speak for yourself," Letch said. "I'm scared for my life."

———

I ate dinner at my friend Skyler's house at least once a week. It was just him and his mom; his dad lived in Denver. His mom was really nice, told me to call her by her first name, Madeline. She let me cook with her. She taught me how to flip an omelet. How to cook a grilled cheese slowly, so everything melted without the bread burning.

And she didn't thaw anything. All the ingredients were fresh.

———

I'd made meatballs with her. We chopped onions and garlic. She said, "You're a natural in the kitchen," and I said, "Really?" and she said, "I'm cooking with a future chef."

We rolled the meat into little globes and put them in the oven.

She drank wine, not from a box, but red wine from a bottle.

"Do you think I could cook these for my mom?"

"She'll love it."

"Really?"

"Of course she will."

———

When they were ready, me, Skyler, and his mom sat around and devoured the meatballs.

"Aren't they delicious?" she asked us.

"I love them," I said, smiling at her.

"They're fine," he said, not looking up from his plate.

———

I'd given my mom a shopping list, and she'd gotten everything I needed. I diced garlic, and they watched me.

"Look at Rhonda," Letch said, "putting his balls into cooking."

"No thawing!" I said.

"Whose son are you?" my mom said, rubbing her arthritic wrists and taking another pain pill. She'd spent the afternoon trying to play songs on the keyboard, and she wasn't happy with the way they'd sounded, swearing and slugging tcha-bliss. "With my son it's thaw or bust."

"Maybe there was a mix-up at the hospital," Letch said. "You guys don't really look alike."

I dumped the garlic on top of the ground beef and onion. I put a little olive oil like Madeline had told me to do. I mixed everything in a big bowl. I didn't like how the animal squished in my hands, but it would be worth it when we all sat at the table together, laughing and eating.

I rolled the first few, a little bigger than golf balls.

"No mix-up," she said. "He was adopted."

"He wasn't adopted," Letch said. "I thought you found him, abandoned."

"That's right. I found him at a bus stop."

"In a paper bag," he said.

My next meatball wasn't round, shaped like an egg.

She laughed and said, "Do you remember that, baby? When I found you at the bus stop?"

I nodded, kept rolling, rolling faster.

"It must have been cold in that paper bag, Rhonda," Letch said.

"He was shivering when I found him."

"Why do you think his real mom got rid of him?"

My meatballs weren't little spheres anymore, but geometric deformities. Monsters. Odd renovations.

"Maybe she was young," my mom said.

"Maybe she was poor," Letch said.

I rolled the last monster and dumped them all in a pan. I was supposed to use a low heat, but I didn't, wanted to cook them as fast as I could so they'd have to shut up and eat. I dumped oil on top of them and shook the pan around.

"But I'm glad she did it because now this angel is mine," she said, laying an arthritic hand on my shoulder.

"What do you think, Rhonda?" he said.

"About what?" I said.

"Why did your mom leave you at that bus stop?"

The meatballs sizzled. I shook the pan again. "She didn't want me."

"Let's change the subject," my mom said.

"She didn't like spending time with me."

"How was school today?" my mom asked.

"She thought her life would be better if I wasn't around."

Some of the meatballs cracked and broke apart. Some stuck to the bottom. I should have been shaking the pan, but I let it sit there, let the meatballs burn and smoke.

My mom filled up her tcha-bliss.

"Your mom asked you about school."

"School's fine."

"You're burning them," my mom said, grabbing a spatula and moving the meatballs around. Most of them had disintegrated into little clumps. Really smoky now.

"Like mother, like son," Letch said. "I'm sure dinner's going to be fantastic."

"She's not my mother," I said. "Remember?"

"We were only teasing," my mom said.

"Watch your mouth," he said to me.

"Baby," my mom said, "will you set the table?"

She pushed the charred meat around the pan.

"She found me at a bus stop, remember?"

"Knock it off," he said.

"No fighting," she said.

Letch glared at me while I set plates, forks, and paper towels on the table. I thought he was going to lose his temper, but he didn't.

"I lost my appetite," he said, walking out of the kitchen and into the garage.

My mom looked at me with a phony smile. She brought the pan over and pushed meat onto our plates. Some of it was burned, some still vaguely pink, none of it edible. We sat down. Neither of us picked up our forks.

"Sorry," she said.

"What for?"

She grabbed my hand and brought it to her mouth. She kissed it. "Do you want me to thaw some taquitos?"

She set our plates in the sink and walked over to the freezer, opened it, and said, "Damn. No taquitos." She pursed her lips. She shut the freezer and peeked in the refrigerator and shook her head. Then she opened a cupboard. "You want some chips?"

"Can we go to Burger King?"

"I've been drinking, baby, and I'm still on probation. I can't drive."

She brought the bag of barbecued chips over and set it between us.

She said, "*Voilà*, dinner is served."

She said, "Come on, baby. Smile for me."

I tried.

PRUNO

The guy was saying how I'd cheated him in a game of pool, months earlier, and that he'd been hoping our paths would cross again, that he'd been coming back to Damascus waiting for me to slither in so he could settle the score.

I asked him, "What score?"

I said, "How can there be a score if I've never seen you in my whole life?"

He ran over to the pool table and snatched a cue stick and tried to hit me in the face with it, but I'd brought my arms up for protection and he hit me in the forearm. The stick shattered, and I buckled to the floor. It hurt so bad that I knew it was broken. Mewling in anguish. There were five or six other people in the bar, but no one was going to get in this guy's way, not when he had that rabid look in his eyes. Not even Vern.

The guy stood over me, saying, "See? See? See how things have a way of coming full circle?" He screamed for a couple minutes, asked if anyone else wished to "bump with the champ." I, to this day, don't remember wishing to bump with the champ. Since no one responded to his universal threat, he walked out.

A couple men helped me off of the floor and got me on a barstool.

"We're going to need whiskey," one of them told the bartender. "Stat!"

I told them my arm was busted and they asked if I wanted to go to the ER and I said, "Are any of you giving me health insurance for Christmas?"

They laughed and muttered and paid for two more whiskeys, but there was no way I could handle ER bills. I would wait for my arm to heal *au naturel.*

———

The guys asked about my arm every time I walked into Damascus.

They would stare at it, disbelieving. "You've gotta have that bone set. It's curving like a huge banana."

A week later, they told me it was getting worse. They couldn't believe the bruising, the harsh, dark colors that looked like burned bacon under my skin. They said that I had to go to the hospital, with or without insurance, like it or not, and that I had to do something before it got so bad that it couldn't be fixed.

Three weeks later, Vern said, "Pretty soon it'll be a boomerang."

"At least my drink will be closer to my face," I said, launching into a loud complaint about money. As in, I was almost out of it. As in, how was I supposed to work the line with a broken arm?

"Pruno," Vern said.

"What?"

"Pruno. Prison wine. I learned how to make it in Lompoc. You'll save money because you won't be paying for drinks."

That was the thing I loved about Damascus: the resource-fulness of the clientele. Solutions for people who didn't want to solve any of their problems, only postpone them. Hide from them. We plastered ourselves in sad disguises.

"How do I make it?" I said.

———

Since I was still out of work, I decided to lower my rent and move into a pay-by-the-week hotel, on Valencia and 15th Street. In the late afternoon, Vern showed up at my new digs with a plastic bag full of supplies to concoct his guerilla-hooch: ten oranges, a can of fruit cocktail, fifty sugar cubes, eight packets of Ketchup from Burger King. He also had a box of red wine for us to drink while he taught me the recipe.

"My mom used to drink this shit," I said, telling Vern how she drank boxes and boxes of tcha-bliss. I thanked him for bringing the wine, told him I couldn't give him any money for it.

"Pay me back in free pruno," he said. He unloaded everything from the plastic bag. "First we have to peel these oranges."

Over the next ten minutes we stripped them all, tossed the fruit in the plastic bag and the peels in the trash. Vern dumped the fruit cocktail in the bag and sealed it.

"You have a family?" he asked.

"Do you?"

"Wife and daughter."

"How old's your little girl?" I said.

"Shit," he said, pausing. "I can't remember. Thirty-nine. No, forty-six."

"What year was she born?"

"1955," he said, pausing again, twirling a mangy eyebrow. "That can't be. '59. '69. '47. No – "

"You two are close."

"Fuck you."

The look on his face told me he was still trying to figure out what year she was born.

"I always wanted a daughter," he said, smashing the fruit with his fists, the bag filling with a paste the color of a jack-o-lantern. "But once I had one, I sure made a mess of it." He took the plastic bag over to the sink and ran it under hot water.

"Do you ever see her?"

He wagged his head fast, the way a shark shakes its food in its mouth, and spoke in the softest voice I'd ever heard him use: "I need to wrap this in something."

"What?"

He found his usual, livid tone. "Just get me a towel!"

"How about a T-shirt?"

"Fine," he said. I handed it to him and he swaddled the bag of pruno in it. He stuck it on a shelf, on a nest of stray, uncooked spaghetti.

We stood, staring at the pruno like proud fathers.

"Is that it?" I said.

"That's day one. It takes a week to make pruno."

"A week?" I whined.

Vern poured me another glass of box wine and shrugged his shoulders. "That saying about how long it took to build Rome," he said, "well it applies to pruno, too."

————

That night, I woke up from my normal nightmare because I heard screaming outside my building. I'd been tossing and turning anyway, because of my arm, the way it throbbed, the way it took the buzzing feeling that had plagued me for years and turned it into a constant agony.

I ran to the window, and a guy dragged a couch into the middle of the street. A woman followed him, begging him to stop. They had come out of my building, but I'd never seen either of them before.

"I can change my ways," she said to him. "You don't have to do this."

"I obviously do," he said. "You can't sit on the couch all day and night. You can't watch TV your whole god damn life."

The guy had stashed a bottle of lighter fluid on the couch, and now he doused it until the container was empty.

"What about company?" the woman said. "Your sister? Where are we going to sit when your sister comes over?"

He pulled out a match and threw it, flames erupting.

I stood by the window, chain-smoking, watching that woman try to save the couch. She ran up to her apartment and came back down to dump pots and pans full of water on the blaze. I thought about helping her, but my broken arm wouldn't let me be of much use. The fire department never came. The amazing thing was the woman's determination; she spent half an hour trying to save it, but the couch was ruined. Once the fire was out, she dragged its smoking carcass near the curb and sat down on it.

I could hear her sobbing. I walked down. A one-legged pigeon hopped around on its foot, flying away as I came past. "Can I sit with you?"

"It's still kind of hot," she said, "but I don't mind if you join me."

She was probably sixty years old. Her hair was gray and thin and really long. It dangled all the way down to her butt and looked like a fraying cape.

I plopped down next to her on the couch. It was wet, smeared in black. My ass and thighs got soaked, but it wasn't as warm as I expected. The look on her face told me that this couch had meant a lot to her. "What's your name?" I said.

"Rhonda."

"Me, too."

She looked at me and laughed. "I've never met a Rhonda with an Adam's apple before."

"Even in San Francisco?"

We both smiled, didn't say anything. For a few minutes we sat there, peering out at the dark street. Every once in a while a car went by, and the people stared at us. The rickety wheels of a stolen shopping cart worked their way down the street, so I turned to look. An old man with an unruly beard, muscular arms. He pushed one shopping cart and towed another one behind him, by connecting a bungee cord from the cart to the back of his belt. As he got close to us, he said, "That's what I call being on the hot seat," and smiled, disappearing toward the Castro and lower Haight districts.

"What happened to your arm?" she said.

I looked down at its mess and tried to wiggle my fingers back and forth. The ring finger was dead. "Why'd he burn your couch?"

"There isn't a reason," old lady Rhonda said. "Sometimes there aren't reasons."

"You can keep it at my place," I said. "I don't have a couch. You can come over and sit on it whenever you want."

We dragged its smoldering skeleton up one flight of stairs. It wasn't easy and it took a long time but we both seemed to be having fun. I couldn't help but wonder when the last time I actually helped somebody was, and when I realized it was Karla, I wished she could see me now.

———

The next afternoon, I went to see the Jordanian Girl. As I walked up to the store, she stood in the doorway, smoking. It looked like she was deep in a daydream; I wanted to ask her what she fantasized about, but I knew she'd never tell me the truth.

"Hi, Big Boy," she said.

"How have you been?"

"Dying from all the excitement." She dropped her cigarette and put it out with her shoe, leaned down and picked up the butt. She walked into the store, and I followed her. "I'm having one of those days where I want to pull the bedspread over my head and scream for hours. Do you know what I mean?"

Me, Rhonda, I knew exactly what she meant. "I've been there."

"Where?"

"That place where life seems easy for everyone, except you."

"Exactly," she said, nodding. "Anyway, how are things going?"

"I need some Magnums."

"Oohhhh." She winked at me. "Some afternoon fun, huh?"

"Yeah."

"It doesn't sound like you're having such a tough life."

"It is," I said and strained to smile. She set the condoms in front of me. She wore a turquoise ring. Her wrists were hairy. I could see her bellybutton, and I'd have given anything to touch it.

"Take any good pictures lately?"

"Not really."

"I was thinking about you because my neighbor feeds the pigeons every morning. There's always a bunch of them waiting for her. You should come by and snap some pics."

"That would be great."

"I'm off on Sundays. I'll give you my address, if you promise you're no stalker."

"Would a stalker admit it?"

"Good point. Guess I'll have to trust you."

————

I left the liquor store and walked down 22nd Street toward Valencia, past the Lone Palm, a bar that actually had one miserable palm tree in front of it, crammed into a tiny planter filled with cigarette butts. There was a cardboard box full of empty liquor bottles sitting on the planter's edge, for the homeless to collect and recycle for a few bucks. I stepped on another sidewalk-stenciling, this one in yellow spray paint: *Homeland security, the resuscitation of fascism.*

When I reached Valencia, the construction work had traffic backed up. They attempted to funnel both directions into a single, alternating lane: one way moved, while the other sat still. Drivers knew if it was their turn to go or not because two construction workers – one in charge of each direction – held a sign, one side yellow and saying *Slow*; the other side, red, told drivers *Stop*. The men radioed back and forth, making sure they had their signals straight.

I walked pretty close to one of the sign-holding men. He seemed to be confused, or overtired, or coddling an awful hangover, because he held the sign so it said *Stop* to the drivers, but with his free hand, he motioned for the cars to move forward. No need to worry, I thought. There was plenty of time for him to turn things around.

The last thing I saw as I walked past all the workers was three men with shovels, who were only visible from their waists up, standing in narrow trenches and looking like gravediggers.

WHAT COULD BE MORE IMPORTANT

After school, Skyler and I used to ride our bikes to a stretch of empty road. We both lived on the edge of Phoenix, where there were miles and miles of desert on the other side of our houses. We'd ride our bikes to a road that no one really used, where the rattlesnakes would lie on the asphalt in the late afternoon, to soak up the sun.

We'd heard that rattlesnakes could only strike if they were coiled, so we felt pretty safe running over their stretched out bodies with our bikes. I don't remember who told us that. I don't know if it's even true. But sometimes, we could run over five or six at a time. Skyler held the record. Eight.

After we hit them, the snakes would purr and open their irate mouths. Some would take off for the sand. Some would coil, scream, dare us to come by again.

Today, though, we hadn't hit any yet, sitting on our bikes and watching them lie there.

"Can I have dinner at your house tonight?" I said.

"I'll have to ask my mom. Do you want to hit them first?"

I smiled and pedaled toward the snakes. One of them was really long, maybe six feet. I hit it, swerved to miss the rest. I said to Skyler, "You see the size of that one?" but the snake had coiled up, making it hard to tell how long it was.

Skyler could go faster than me. He didn't pedal near the one I'd hit, but smashed three other snakes underneath his tires.

We sat on our bikes some more, watching the snakes act all ballistic.

"It's my birthday," I said. It really was.

"Mom get you anything?"

"I'll see later."

"Forget about asking my mom," Skyler said. "Come eat dinner."

———

When we got to his house, Skyler's mom was unloading groceries. He told her it was my birthday. She hugged me, picked up her car keys, and said, "Forget what I was going to make for dinner, what would the birthday boy like?"

"Whatever you were going to make is fine," I said.

"No way, José. Now what's it going to be?"

A couple weeks before, she'd taught me how to make her very own recipe: ground meat mixed with broccoli and tomato sauce. "Meat Trees?" I said, not really caring what we cooked, as long as we made it together.

"You liked my Meat Trees?"

"Loved them."

"Are you sure it's okay with your mom that you stay?"

"She said it's fine," Skyler said to her. "She's got a lot of work tonight."

Madeline pursed her lips. "You guys go play, while I go back to the store."

———

I wasn't really paying attention, as Skyler and I sat in his room, fiddling with little motorcycles. I was listening for his mom to come back.

As soon as she did, I said to Skyler, "I'm going to help her cook."

"I figured. I'm going to stay here."

I ran to the kitchen. "What can I do?"

"You don't have to do anything. Play with Sky."

"Please?"

"If you insist," she said, putting her hand on my head. We set all the ingredients out on the counter. "Should I call your mom and see if she wants to come to dinner?"

"She's real busy."

Madeline coughed. "But wouldn't you like her to try Meat Trees?" She handed me a knife, and I started hacking up an onion. "What did she get you for your birthday?"

"It's a surprise when I get home."

"Are you sure your mom wouldn't want to eat with us?"

"She can't."

"I'm going to call over there."

"She's real busy."

"I'm just going to ask. Is that all right, sweetie?" Madeline dialed.

I kept cutting the onion into smaller and smaller pieces. My eyes burned.

She kept the phone to her ear and said, "No answer."

"She's probably too busy to pick up right now. Should I chop the garlic, too?"

"Yes, please."

I chopped away. She seasoned the ground meat with salt, pepper, Worcestershire. Skyler came in and asked how long until dinner was ready and she said twenty minutes. Madeline told me she'd be back in a minute, that she needed to talk to Sky really fast. They went into his room. I heard the door shut. I put the knife down and snuck over, listened with my ear pressed against it.

"I want to know where his mother is," she said. "I know she's not working."

"She is so."

"What could be more important than his birthday?" and when she said that, I didn't want to hear anything else. I didn't want to chop garlic or cook Meat Trees. I didn't want anything except to be by myself, so I snuck out through the garage and rode my bike home.

―――

My mom wasn't there. Neither was Letch. I went into my room and loved myself. The phone rang, but I didn't answer it.

―――

About forty-five minutes later, someone knocked on the front door. Someone rang the doorbell. I waited a while before I went and peeked to see who was standing there, but they were long gone. I unlocked it, opened it. Sitting on the ground was a Tupperware container with a note on top. It said, "Happy birthday. Your friends, Skyler and Madeline."

I locked the front door again and took the Tupperware in my room. I ate every last speck before I went to watch TV.

DOWN HERE

Little-Rhonda and I sat on the burned couch, killing time. He'd come back a couple hours earlier, after I'd gotten home from seeing the Jordanian Girl. "I need you to dig down into the dumpster again."

The hand connected to my good arm got a grinding feeling, like a mill crushing peppercorns. "When?"

"Soon."

"Now?"

"After that crap-shack taqueria shuts down for the night," he said. "We don't want the hired help harassing you again." He turned his helmet's light off. "And speaking of harassment, what's with this disgusting couch?"

I told him the whole story, old lady Rhonda, her pyromaniac husband.

"But what's it doing in your apartment?" he asked.

"I'm keeping it for her. In case she wants to visit it."

"Visit a couch?" He looked at me like Karla had, horrified, appalled at my aptitude to do the wrong thing. "Are you listening to yourself?"

I was trying; we sat there until one a.m.

———

The dumpster was three-quarters full. There wasn't as much food in it tonight as the last time. It had more napkins and to-go boxes, which made it easier for me to toss everything out and into the alley.

"Why don't you ever help with this part?" I said to little-Rhonda.

He shrugged, leaning against the dumpster, smoking. The light on his helmet was on. "You're the brawn, I'm the brains." He laughed. "Correction: the one-armed brawn."

I felt a few raindrops. It was weird to get rain in San Francisco before Halloween. I finished pitching everything out of the dumpster and opened the door in its bottom.

"After you," I said to little-Rhonda. He hopped in the dumpster and took off down the ladder. In a matter of seconds, I couldn't see him.

I hadn't really thought about how I was going to climb down a ladder with a broken arm until now. It was easier than I thought, as long as I kept my weight leaning into it and going really slowly. I called after little-Rhonda, "I need your help," and he said, "I know that," and I said, "I don't think you know what I mean," and he said, "I know exactly what you mean."

By the time I got to the bottom, all sweaty, he was up against a wall and smoking again. "You aren't exactly in tip-top shape," he said.

"You climb down a ladder with one arm."

"Poor you," little-Rhonda said. "We'll have to sign you up for the Special Olympics."

I rested for a minute, then walked through the dark tunnel. The hand I'd used to make my way down the ladder had a couple blisters across its palm that looked like albino ants.

"You have to go in by yourself this time," he said.

"Why?"

"I'll wait right here."

I went inside. It was still empty, except for a box of my mom's wine way over in a corner. I wended to it, pushed the spout and tcha-bliss dribbled out, not running in a random pattern, but forming a Rorschach-puddle. I dove into it, and as I fell, its color got darker and darker, and soon it was pitch black like the other puddle had been. I fell for longer this time, what seemed hours. I kept my eyes open but couldn't see a foot in front of me. Then the invisible parachute slowed me down again, and I landed on the window where I could see my mom and little-Rhonda on the other side. They were in the kitchen. He wasn't wearing his helmet. She played her Casio keyboard. She used to be a great pianist, before I was born, before her rheumatoid arthritis turned her hands into stupid fruit. She tried to make a run up the keys and missed some notes, took a swig of tcha-bliss, and said to him, "Not exactly how Mozart drew it up," and he said, "I like it," and she said, "You're always such a charmer." She kept playing, fingers fumbling across the keys. It was one of those keyboards that wasn't full-sized, only three octaves total. She said, "You won't know until you get older, baby, but it's awful to falter at something you used to be great at."

I stared down at them, at the way he stared up at her, at the way she scowled at the keyboard, at the malicious way she grabbed the tcha-bliss. "Are your hands hurting right now?" he said, and she said, "These days, they always are," and he said, "Will you play my favorite Vivaldo song?" and she smiled and said, "Vivaldi?" and he smiled, too, saying, "Yeah, Vivaldi."

I hadn't heard her play in so long. Me, Rhonda, lying down on the glass, ear smashed into it, wanting to hear her perform. Her fingers moved slowly, pressing horrible sounding combinations of keys. But the boy stared up at her in awe. She winced when she needed to stretch her fingers to reach certain notes, which she missed anyway. Then she stopped playing, let her clumsy hands crash in her lap. She turned the keyboard off, saying, "What's the point?"

"It sounds great."

There was only a sip left of her tcha-bliss. "You shouldn't lie to your mother."

———

I went over to the Jordanian Girl's house that Sunday. Around ten a.m. Nervous. I had the same disposable camera as before, since it still had nine pictures remaining.

True to the Jordanian Girl's word, a woman sat on the front steps, tearing bread into bits and feeding the pigeons, maybe twenty of them competing for crumbs.

"Hi," I said to the woman, panicking when I realized I didn't know what the Jordanian Girl's name was and wanting to ask the neighbor if she was home. My good hand buzzed.

"Honda!" the woman yelled, over her shoulder, toward the house. "Your friend is here."

Honda? Honda and Rhonda? It was too good to be true. Or it was just good. Or just true. It was something, whatever it was, that I was unfamiliar with.

She came outside.

"Honda?" I said. "Your parents must really love cars."

"It's spelled *H-A-N-D-A*. My father drives an Audi." She pointed at all the pigeons. "Looks like this is your lucky day."

"Our lucky day," I said. "My name is Rhonda."

"Isn't that a girl's name?"

"Family tradition."

"Handa and Rhonda," she said and laughed. "What are the chances?"

I didn't want to answer that question. I put the camera to my eye.

"What do you do with your pictures?" Handa asked.

"Huh?"

"Your pigeon pictures. Do you sell them, hang them in galleries?"

I wound the disposable camera, took a shot of three pigeons fighting for the same piece of bread. The neighbor's feet were in the picture, too, bare, with overgrown toenails. "They're just for me. It's only a hobby."

"I wish I was like you."

"What do you mean?"

"An *artiste*?" she said in a terrible French accent. It sounded like her tongue had swollen up to the size of a pancake.

I wound again and snapped another shot, this one of a white pigeon, off by himself, watching the others wriggle. "I'm no artist."

"All I do is sleep and work, sleep and work. At least your life has a passion."

I thought about my mom, her Casio keyboard. The murder in her eyes every time she hit awkward combinations of keys. "I'm not any good."

"Even if you aren't, so what? You're doing something."

"Here," I said, handing her the camera. "Try it."

"I can't."

"Even if you aren't any good, so what?" I said, smiling. She took it from me.

"I don't want to take pictures of the ugly birds." She pointed the camera at me. "Make a sexy face."

"I am."

"Try harder." I heard the camera click. When was the last time someone had taken my picture? I gave her a huge, exaggerated smile. "Never mind," she said. "Try less hard."

"Can I please have that back?"

"Don't be a baby," she said, and we laughed, her laughter more sincere, mine shrouded in the memory of Karla saying *pathetic little baby*. Mine masked because one minute, I was a hero, and the next, she threw me out of her house, her life.

Again, I aimed the camera at the throng of pigeons. Shot two more. Wound the camera to take another, but I was out of film. "That's all for now."

"Already?" Handa said, and with the wretched French accent, her pancake-tongue, "I was enjoying watching an *artiste* work."

"Let's get together again."

"Come by the store soon."

She wanted me, Rhonda, to come by the store. Handa and Rhonda. On my way home, I dropped the camera off to get the film developed.

❋

CRASH MAN

The next night, Vern came by a little after midnight to work on the pruno. He unwrapped it from the T-shirt. Gases had made the plastic bag swell up, pregnant. He opened it and dumped in all those sugar cubes, squeezed in the packets of ketchup, and added some water.

"Are you going to tell me or what?" he said.

"The couch?"

"Yes, the fucking couch," he said, licking some ketchup from his finger.

"It belongs to a friend," I said, and right when I was about to tell him the whole story, I heard the guy's voice again. Old lady Rhonda's husband. Screaming. Walking out front of our building. I ran over to the window, and there he was, carrying a TV out into the middle of the street. Old lady Rhonda was more aggressive in her defense of the television, punching her husband in the back.

"Live your own life!" the guy was saying. "Stop watching other people live on TV!"

"Please don't do this," she said.

Vern stood next to me at the window.

"We have to help her," I said.

"I don't do that damsel-in-distress thing."

"My arm is busted. I need your help."

"You go. I'll tend to the pruno."

"We have to help her."

Vern glared at me. "Look, I like you. We're friends, right? But did I get off my barstool when that guy hit you with a cue stick? Did I come save you? No. Why would I help some woman I don't even know?"

"I'm going," I said and took off down the stairs and came out onto the street right when the guy drenched the TV in lighter fluid.

"Hey!" I barked at him, feeling all heroic. I looked at my bent arm, wondering what I'd do to defend myself if he wanted to tussle.

"Don't," old lady Rhonda said to me. She looked really scared, and her frightened eyes made me remember Karla and the way the man's wedding ring had punctured my nose, the taste of blood slipping down my throat, me crumpled up on the sidewalk after he kicked me and strutted away.

"Who are you?" the guy said. He had huge front teeth, the size of playing cards.

"You don't have to burn the TV," I said. I looked at my good hand. Worrying about a fistfight. It looked so small and useless. Like I saw an ultrasound of myself. Me, Rhonda, a fetus. Me, with the buzzing fetus hand. "Just give it away. Give it to me. I don't have one."

"I'm teaching her a lesson," he said.

"It's the same lesson. Either way she doesn't have the TV."

The guy mulled my offer over for a minute. You could tell that he really wanted to burn something and was disappointed that there might be another way to solve the problem. I was sure he'd incinerate it anyway. But finally he agreed to give it to me, and old lady Rhonda kept thanking him and he was saying, "Yeah, yeah," while walking back into our building. She looked at me and winked. I shot one back at her.

––––––

When I got done struggling up the stairs with the TV, I kicked my front door until Vern opened it.

"I wouldn't light a cigarette too close to this idiot box," Vern said, "unless you want to burn the place down."

"Will you help me?"

He sighed and grabbed a side of the TV, relieving my crooked arm of the excruciating weight. We walked in and set it on the couch.

"I'm proud of you," Vern said.

"Are you teasing?"

"No, seriously. I thought that guy was gonna burn it for sure."

"Thanks."

"Let's not get all sappy, soldier," he said and walked straight to the door and left.

———

I kept peeking at the pruno. Nothing had really changed since Vern added the ketchup, water, and sugar cubes. The bag had lost all of its pressure that had made it swell so big before, but it was showing signs of bulging again slightly around the edges, beads of condensation collecting on the inside of the bag.

I couldn't tell you why, but I kept getting out of bed every couple of hours, walking into the kitchen and checking on the pruno. Making sure everything was all right.

Finally, about five a.m. I snatched the pruno off of its nest of spaghetti crumbs in the kitchen and set it down on the floor next to my mattress. I sent the klutzy, dying hand from my bent arm over to touch the pruno every time I stirred in my sleep.

———

Two nights later, old lady Rhonda and I were on the burned couch, watching "Wheel of Fortune." A man from Boise, Idaho, spun the wheel and lost everything. BANKRUPT! Pat Sajak shook his head like he was astonished; he apologized to the man and said, "There's more where that came from."

The couch had dried out nicely. It smelled like singed hair and mold, but neither of us minded. Old lady Rhonda brought American cheese sandwiches and a bottle of cheap vodka, which we drank on the rocks, out of coffee cups. I'd backwashed a big piece of sandwich crust into my drink, and it sat on the bottom like a decomposing fish. Her long gray hair was pulled into a pony tail. It was the only one I'd ever seen that actually looked like a horse's tail.

On the TV: two words: a person:

C_A_ _ _AN _A_

"Figure it out yet?" old lady Rhonda said.

"Not yet." I tried to grab that piece of crust from my cocktail, but it only broke up, lying in brown clumps.

A guy on TV said, "Is there an *L*?"

"No, *L*," Pat Sajak said.

"I've already got it," old lady Rhonda said to me. "I'm not good at much, but 'Wheel of Fortune' is my game."

"What is it?"

"I'm not telling," she said.

TV: "Is there a *W*?"

Pat Sajak: "No *W*."

"Have you ever thought about going on the show?" I asked her.

"I'd probably freeze up. Stand there looking stupid. That's what my husband says, anyway."

"Fuck him," I said.

TV: "An *M*?"

Pat Sajak: "Yes."

Vanna White walked over and touched the *M*'s illuminated spaces.

C_A_ _ MAN MA_

"Got it yet?" Rhonda said.

I was convinced. "Yes."

"What is it?"

"Crash man," I said.

"What the hell's a crash man?"

"It's like a stunt man who deals exclusively with crashes."

"There's no such thing," old lady Rhonda said, "and besides, look at the TV again. That wouldn't say crash man. It would say *Crashman Man*."

I got up and finished my drink and went to the fridge for some more ice cubes. I dumped them in without rinsing the backwash out of my glass.

"Are you sulking?" she said.

"No." But I might have been. I drank an entire glassful of vodka before filling it again and coming back to the couch.

"I got to go," old lady Rhonda said. "Got to have dinner ready before my husband gets home from work."

"Is he good to you?"

She looked at me, her lips pursed. "What do you mean?"

"Is he nice?"

"When he's not burning my stuff, sure, he's nice."

"What are you doing in the morning?"

"No plans," she said.

"Let's have breakfast."

She hugged me. "You ask if he's nice, but no one's been as nice to me as you are in years. Do you like waffles?"

I nodded. We were still hugging.

"I'll cook a masterpiece," old lady Rhonda said.

"Any time you want, you can come and sit on the couch if you miss it."

"It isn't that I love this couch," she pointed toward the window, "it's that I hate it out there."

We kept hugging. I didn't want it to stop, but I could feel her arms go heavy, waiting to pull away. I squeezed her one more time, and we walked to the front door.

"Oh, and the answer to the puzzle is *Chairman Mao*," she said, smiling. "My little Crash Man."

TELL ME MORE

I'd like to hear more about the house, he said. The weird thing was I never saw Angel-Hair eat any tuna fish, just the smell, always the smell. I didn't know what else to tell him, I'd been saying the same stories for days, months, years. I said, It was all that house's fault. How is it the house's fault, he asked. The house, I said. No question, I said. Angel-Hair sat in front of me. His left leg crossed over the right one. It went black shoe, black sock, streak of white leg, black pants. I could look over his head and through the metal grating and out the window and I could see the desert sky. Letch and I used to shoot doves out of the same sky with twelve-gauge shotguns. Teaching Rhonda to be a man, he said. Angel-Hair's eyes popped back and forth, focusing on my left eye then my right eye. Letch wanted to go to Vietnam, but both his kidneys were on the same side of his body, and he wasn't allowed to go and kill. How could it be the house's fault, Angel-Hair asked. But I knew the house was cursed. It was the place where the men, all the men that mom loved, they came in the house, stayed in the house, all the men who were never nice, hurting us, leaving us. All the wrong notes she hit on her keyboard. The house is evil, I said. How, he said. Right eye. The sidewinders were my friends, but Letch had introduced us. One day. While we were shooting doves. He found one coiled and purring. Letch knew how to pick it up without getting bitten. Sometimes the doves didn't die when you shot them. They'd flop on the sand. One of their wings going crazy. You had to take them by the heads and spin their bodies around in circles to break their necks. Letch picked up the snake, first by the tail and then he somehow took hold of it right behind its head. I was scared, just watching him do it. But I was also hoping. What if, I thought. What if that snake sticks him full of poison. Left eye. The doctor leaned down and scratched the plot of white skin that was above the black shoe, the black sock. Letch held the snake and said, Come over here, Rhonda. Angel-Hair said, Please tell me how the house was evil. The sidewinder was hissing and screaming. Its fangs were out. I didn't want to go anywhere near it. Look, Letch said, wagging the snake. I inched toward them. Closer, Rhonda, he said. I won't let anything happen to you, he said. The doctor coughed. I'm waiting for an answer, he said. What was the question, I said, and he said, How was the house evil. The house was evil because it was the place where all the bad stuff happened. But the house, he said, didn't do the bad stuff. I didn't answer him. Started wondering whether that house was cursed forever, wondering if every little kid who lived there would be shattered like me. Sometimes after we killed doves, I'd get a splotchy bruise on my right shoulder, from the kick of the shotgun. Letch would press on it. Tease me. He'd say, Mark of a man. I liked it when he said that. He held the sidewinder up, at my eye level. He said, I want you to stick your face right in there. Why, I said, and he said, Do it. I said to Angel-Hair, Some places are just cursed. Letch, really yelling now, shook the snake around, agitating it. Hissing and screaming. Right eye. God damnit, Rhonda, he said. I want you close enough to kiss it, he said. I knew not to cry. I knew that there wasn't anything I could say to change his mind. Will you hold it still, I said. He smiled. He said, That a boy. And then Letch wasn't moving the snake at all, holding it perfectly still, but the sidewinder's mouth was wide open, fangs gleaming. Purring like crazy. I stuck my face right in there, inches away. Its breath smelled like lighter fluid. Talk to it, Letch said. I'm not scared of you, I said. Good, Letch

said, Say it again. I'm not scared of you. I'm not scared of you.
I'm not scared of you. I'm not scared of you. You can't blame
the house, Angel-Hair said. But I could. I could blame anything.
Anyone. I wasn't through with that house yet.

ONE RED LEG

The next morning, old lady Rhonda showed up at my apartment with some groceries and a beat-up waffle iron. I sat on the kitchen counter, and we drank mimosas. I'd been sitting in the kitchen anyway, before she got there, staring at the picture of the homeless man with the splayed pizza box on his face that I'd taped to the refrigerator. My miracle. My reminder that things could be worse. I tried explaining it to her.

"Why do you need to be reminded of that?" old lady Rhonda said.

"I don't know. Perspective?"

"Bullshit," she said. "You don't need to know that things can be worse, Crash Man. What you need to know is that they can be better!" She made chocolate chip waffles and over-easy eggs. We gorged and lurched to the burned couch, smoking cigarettes. Then she asked me if I had a job.

"Not right now. Because of this," I said, holding up my crooked arm.

"You should get that fixed."

"It's not that simple."

"It's extremely simple."

Me, Rhonda, not knowing what to say, not saying anything, because I should have gotten it fixed, I should have wanted to get it fixed, but I didn't care. It was crooked and so what? Lots of things in life lost their shape. I thought about all of the pigeon-amputees who hopped around the Mission district on one spindly, red leg.

"I'll fix it soon."

"When?"

"When I'm not broke."

"But it's broke."

I didn't answer.

She reached over and rubbed my leg, letting me off the hook: "You want another cigarette?"

I nodded and she handed me one. I lit it, took a drag.

"Do you have a girlfriend?" she said.

"Not right now."

"We have to get you one."

"We have to get you a nice husband."

She laughed. "He isn't always like that."

"Do you want me to talk to him?"

"No one can talk to him."

"I'm not afraid."

"I can tell," she said, leaning over and pushing her hand through my curly hair. "You were so brave, the way you saved my TV. I don't want to talk about him right now. Do you want something else to eat?"

I was full. But I'd never say no to her. "Can I have another waffle?"

"Where do you put all this food, skinny boy?" She walked into the kitchen, plugged the waffle iron back in, poured more batter into the old machine. It wheezed sickly clouds of steam from its sides.

"Do you guys have any kids?"

"He said we'd have them. Promised we'd have them. But he always had a reason why we should wait. And then one day we were old."

"I'm sorry."

"Is there a girl you like?"

I thought of Handa. That swirl of hairs around her belly-button. How she made me go sweaty and edgy and nervous, as if she was an amphetamine. The way she'd smiled when she'd first called me *Big Boy*. "I'm getting up the guts to ask someone out."

"Who?"

"She works at the liquor store at 22nd and Dolores."

Old lady Rhonda jerked another chocolate chip waffle out of the steaming machine, slid it on a plate, and doused it in syrup. She handed it to me. "Why haven't you asked her out yet?"

"Scared, I guess."

"I'm not one for giving advice. But one thing I learned in my life is that you have to go after the things that mean something to you. What you want never comes without a fight." She frowned, pointed toward the ceiling, her apartment, her husband. Her grimace got more severe. "I guess I didn't actually learn that lesson, but I should have."

I took a bite of waffle. "I'll ask her out soon."

"Soon," she scoffed. "Like your arm?" She didn't say it in a nagging way, but like she really cared.

"You should have had kids," I said. "You'd have been a great mother."

"That's the nicest thing anyone has said to me in years. With all your charm, I think you should ask that girl out this week."

"I don't know."

"What's the worse thing that can happen?"

I thought about Karla grabbing my hand and shoving it into my wet crotch, calling me *pathetic little baby*. "Maybe I'll ask her." I finished my waffle, my mimosa, my cigarette. "I'll think about it."

"Will you do it for me?" Old lady Rhonda took my empty plate to the kitchen. She handed me another cigarette when she came back and sat down. "I'm not trying to pressure you. I just think it will do you some good to get a girlfriend." She smiled. "Okay, fine, maybe I'm trying to pressure you a little bit."

I'd have done anything she asked. "I'll do it this week."

"Good boy. Another mimosa?"

"No thanks."

"But the orange juice has so much vitamin C. Will you please have one more?" She told me to finish the last sip of my mimosa so she could make me another. I tipped the coffee cup way back, killing the last of it, and she said, "It's almost flu season so we need all the vitamins we can get." Then old lady Rhonda walked to the kitchen and poured champagne in my coffee cup, topping it with orange juice, which bubbled up over the top of the mug and spilled all over the counter. "Damn!" she said.

I ran over to the kitchen and slurped mimosa off the counter. "Look at all the precious vitamin C you're wasting," I said. "Will you help me?" and she leaned down, and together, we licked that counter until there wasn't a drop left.

STINGS

When the wasp stung me, my mom got all protective and worried in a way I'd never seen before. I walked in the house, crying, holding the welt on my arm where it had stung me, and she said, "Baby, what happened?" and I told her that I'd been stung and that my skin was all itchy and my throat hurt and that it was hard to breathe. She said, "You must be allergic," and I said, "Am I going to die?" and she said, "I won't let anything bad happen to you."

I'd had colds and the flu tons of times, and she never cared. She'd tell me to stop being so dramatic, it's just the sniffles, grow up. She'd disappear for days. Not call once to ask if I was all right, and when she got home, if I wandered behind her, like a shunned pet, and asked where she'd been, she'd say, "I need to rest. We'll talk later"; but all that happened later was about two gallons of tcha-bliss, missing notes on her keyboard, whining about her arthritis, maybe a fight with Letch.

The wasp sting made her really worry about me. She wet a rag with freezing water and held it on the sting, then my forehead. She rubbed an arthritic hand across my cheek. I kept crying because my skin broke out in a gigantic rash, and she hugged me the whole time.

I kept saying, "You won't let anything happen to me, right?" and she said, "No, baby. I never will."

———

About a month later, the wasp sting was long forgotten and she was up to her old routine of pretending I wasn't there.

She was out of work again, and it was one of those days where she and Letch couldn't stop screaming at each other. I was supposed to be watching TV and minding my own business, but I couldn't concentrate on anything except their warfare in our stretched, sandy house, as they screamed throughout the desert that was everywhere: a cactus had sprouted next to the TV, a dove perched on it; animals flying, slithering, crawling, running all around our house, our desert; animals, livid and territorial.

Letch saw me looking at my mom and him. "Get the hell out of here so we can finish talking, Rhonda."

Then he slapped her.

I'd never seen him hit her before.

He pointed toward the door and told me, "Now."

My mom rubbed her cheek.

I stared at her, wanted to do something to help, but she said, "Just get out, baby."

I ran into the front yard, ran into the street, ran down it. I was running and I couldn't stop thinking how her saying, "Just get out, baby," was the first thing she'd said to me all day, and I got to thinking about the wasp sting, about her holding that wet rag on my forehead, and the next thing I knew, I ran to where the wasp had stung me the first time. I'd seen the nest but thought I could sneak by without bumping it, but I bumped it, and a wasp flew out and attacked, and I was running there now to bump the nest again, to bump it so hard that the wasps had no choice but to defend their home, their family. The nest was stuck to a telephone pole. I took my hand and, like Letch had hit her, slapped the nest. It was only the size of a silver dollar. It was brown. I slapped it and most of it broke off and landed on the sidewalk. Next thing I knew I felt a sting on my shoulder. My heart started pounding. Throat tightening up. I sprinted home so she could see me crying and see the rash exploding all over my skin, its bright violence. She'd wet the rag with freezing water and make sure I was all right.

———

About a month after that, I tried it one more time. She'd just gotten home from another of her disappearing acts; she and Letch were going in circles about who she'd been with this time.

"Just me and Lori," she said, and he said, "Lori my ass."

"I swear it was just the two of us," she said, and he said, "I believe there were two of you, but his name wasn't Lori."

She said, "Seriously, Lori," and he said, "Seriously, Lori my ass," and he hit her again, shaking his head, saying, "Yeah, right, Lori."

I sat in front of the TV, but paid more attention to the desert. We barely had a home anymore. Its rooms had stretched to huge distances. The walls had fire ants all over them. Joshua trees and Gila monsters were in the kitchen. Buzzards in the bedrooms, picking at the dead flesh. And the sidewinders, my bodyguards, always slithering in that impossible *S*-shape of theirs, chasing danger away from me whenever they could.

It was only a matter of time until Letch told me to get the hell out so I left. Went into our backyard. There was now a wasps' nest on the eve of our crappy patio. I'd discovered it a week before and had been waiting for the right time to make one sting me. I almost did it when I first noticed the nest, but my mom was in the middle of her latest disappearing act, and I knew Letch wouldn't care if I'd been stung a thousand times. I imagined myself walking up to him and screaming, "A wasp stung me!" and he'd say, "Sure, Rhonda, I'd love a Bloody Maria, thanks for asking."

I pulled a chair over and stood on it to reach the wasps' nest. I flicked it with my finger. Nothing happened. I flicked it harder. Flicked it like six times. Nothing. I punched the nest and still nothing happened.

The wasps weren't home, and I could hear Letch and my mom screaming, and I didn't know what to do. Was I crying?

I heard Letch yell, "Maybe I'll leave for a while with Lori, too," and my mom said, "Go ahead," and he said, "See you next week," and she said, "Fine by me," and the front door slammed.

I stood on the chair, picking the last flecks of nest off the beam. I didn't want to go back inside without being stung. Then I felt the glorious pinprick of a wasp. On the back of my neck. Immediately, it happened again: the racing heart, the tight throat, skin going all scratchy, splotchy.

I hopped off the chair and said, "Mom! Help!"

I stood there and said, "Mom! A wasp! Help!"

I stood there and I got all dizzy from the sting and my throat was tighter than normal. I could barely breathe. My skin was itchier than the other times, felt like rusty forks were scraping all over my body, almost drawing blood.

I said, "Mom! Help me!"

I ran inside, thinking maybe she couldn't hear, but she was right there, in the kitchen, leaning on a Joshua tree.

"I got stung again."

She didn't say anything, moving away from the tree and trying to get more tcha-bliss from the box by tilting it forward, but only a few drops dripped into her glass. She didn't look at me. She shook the box, but no more wine dribbled out. She finished it in a sip.

"Wet a rag and dab it," she said.

"But it stung me on the back of the neck. I can't reach."

"This is the third time."

"I need your help."

She sighed, held her glass under the box's spout again and started shaking the box around as hard as she could. Nothing came out. Then she threw the box against the wall and it landed in the sand, fire ants crawling all over it.

"Bring me the damn rag," she said.

WRITHING WITH ANGRY LIFE

I should have known better than to try new things. But I'd convinced myself that old lady Rhonda was right, and I should ask out Handa. So I shaved and showered. I listened to little-Rhonda say, "What's going to happen if she sees you with your pants off? Don't you think she might notice you're not exactly Magnum material?"

"You're not helping," I said.

"No, but I'm having a great time."

And despite his wisecracks, I was having a great time, too. I had little-Rhonda and old lady Rhonda and the bag of pruno. I guess, I had Vern, too, though I didn't count him as much a part of my family because I never knew what to expect from him. One minute, he watched me have my arm broken by a cue stick and didn't do anything to help; the next, he gave me the recipe for prison wine.

If I told you I'd named the pruno, would you judge me?

Would you think I was ludicrous?

Well, I named it. Madeline.

I loved having her lie by my bed. I'd see her and I'd think to myself: you are the only person I've ever really taken care of.

———

Little-Rhonda walked with me down Valencia, on our way to Handa's liquor store. A huge stretch of road had been closed – 18th to 22nd Street – and stripped clean of all its asphalt, a barren stretch of dirt. Down the middle of the road, the workers and their machines had dug huge trenches and now guided dangling pipes into the ground, slowly being lowered by thick chains.

I kept trying to send the little fellow back home, but he wouldn't listen. "Do you think you'll smooch her?" he said, snickering.

"Stop it."

"Don't be so sensitive. I'm here for moral support. We both are," he said, and a sidewinder slithered up and sat on his shoulder like a pirate's parrot.

"I don't need your help."

He launched into a vulgar laugh, snorting, flipping his helmet's light off and on as fast as he could. The sidewinder purred. Little-Rhonda said, "You need help like a hobo needs a candied ham."

And then we were right across the street from the liquor store; Handa stood in the doorway, smoking, waving at us.

"Any last words of encouragement?" I said to little-Rhonda, but he was gone.

Halfway across the street, I looked up at the palm trees that ran down the middle of Dolores Street, in a median of dried grass. Wind whipped through their fronds. There was a highchair knocked on its side, sitting beneath one of the hissing trees.

"That arm, Big Boy. Does it hurt?" Handa yelled to me.

I didn't know what to say. It was uncomfortable and I couldn't really move my fingers and I was still adjusting to the little things, like tying my shoes and using a can opener. But the swarming, sizzling way my hand used to feel had vanished since the arm had been broken. Now my hands were opposites of each other: one always feeling, always thrumming; the other one, dead to the world.

I walked up, admiring her curves. "It's not so bad."

"No?"

"It comes in handy. Patting myself on the back."

"That would be nice." She ground out her smoke, leaned down, and picked up the butt, carrying it back in the store. I followed her. Like always, she had about an inch of skin showing between her pants and her shirt. I envied the dark hairs stretching out of the skin above her ass, imagining what it would be like to be a drop of sweat, clinging in that field of lovely hairs.

She sauntered behind the counter. I got as close to my side of it as I could.

"Do you have a date tonight?" she said, turning her body and reaching for the Magnums.

"No," I said, "I came to see you."

"Me?"

We stood there and nothing was going to stop me. Her hand fell away from the condoms.

"What's new?" I said.

Her face lit up. "Hector is new."

"Who's Hector?"

"I've got a new boyfriend. Now you're not the only one having all the good times."

Maybe it was time to accept the fact that all the great codes of the universe were conspiring against me. My good hand went nuts, a hive writhing with angry life.

"Hector is like you," she said.

"What?"

"I shouldn't be telling you this," she said, giggling, "but he's a big boy, too."

I wasn't trying to yell. I hope you know that. My hand had harsh explosions, and suddenly my thoughts were too loud, swelling to gigantic sound waves, my thoughts shouted themselves around my head, like a bat bouncing its sonar off of cave walls. I'm trying to tell you that the noise in my head blared and I yelled to hear myself but I wasn't yelling at her, okay?

"I have to go!" I said.

She cringed, stepped back. "See you next time."

I wasn't trying to yell at her, but my lungs, hanging pink and wet and bloated in my chest like freshly skinned animals, kept filling with huge amounts of air, and shoving massive noises out of me. "I just remembered I'm supposed to meet a friend! I have to leave right now!"

"See you later."

And she had Hector, and I had no one, and I didn't want her to think that I had no one, so I said, "I better get some Magnums just in case! You never know! Have a great day!"

"You, too," she said and rung up the rubbers.

I paid her. I was only trying to hear what I was saying. Nothing more. I would never have intentionally screamed at her. You need to know that. I said, "Thanks!" and walked away fast, rounding the corner, and as soon as I was out of her sight, I took off running to Damascus, only stopping at a trashcan to throw away the condoms.

I ran down Dolores to 20th Street, took a right. Hit Valencia, passing over the dirt trenches on a piece of plywood the construction crew had laid out at the crosswalk for pedestrians and sprinted by La Rondalla, which already smelled like grease and enchilada sauce and they weren't even open yet. Moved across Mission, South Van Ness, Folsom. It was early afternoon. The wind still clipped through the neighborhood, and I saw a toddler walking and holding onto his mother's leg, steadying himself from blowing around the sidewalk like a downed kite.

––––––

Damascus, in the afternoon. You already know the floor, walls, and ceiling had been painted black, but the windows, too, had been smeared in it. During the day, the bartenders made sure that the door was kept closed. It was like a casino, the way Damascus tried to keep daylight away from its patrons, protecting us from the sun: those beams of light that illuminated the secret woes of daytime drinkers.

I walked in, trying to calm myself down. I was sweaty from running, but my thoughts weren't shouts anymore, and the war in my good hand was over. If not over, quiet for the time being and that was enough.

Vern sat at the bar with a Latino, El Salvadoran, I think, a name tattooed across the side of his neck in a faded cursive. I couldn't make out what the name was.

They both drank warm beers. No other customers were in Damascus yet; the bartender shot a game of pool by himself.

I walked over to Vern and his friend.

"This is Enrique," Vern said to me.

He and I shook hands; I tried to shake Vern's, too, but he looked at me and made a farting noise, his little, white tongue waggling in front of his lips.

"I like your tattoo," I said to Enrique.

He ran his fingers over it and laughed in a surprised way. "My Gloria," he said. "I got that on our first wedding anniversary." I looked at his left hand and didn't see a ring. Enrique said he'd be right back, that he was going to play some songs on the jukebox, but really, I think he needed to spend a couple of minutes remembering Gloria.

"Did you drink the pruno yet?" Vern said.

"I need some whiskey."

"Whiskey you shall have, soldier," he said. "Hey!" he yelled at the bartender, who was attempting a bank shot, which he missed and then made a face at Vern like it was his fault.

"What do you want now?" the bartender said.

"This boy's dying of thirst."

"Yeah, yeah." The bartender threw the cue stick on the table and loped behind the bar. I wondered if that was the stick that had broken my arm.

"Now that's stupendous customer service," Vern said.

"Go to hell," the bartender said.

"Devil's prodigal son shall soon return. The day I die, he'll throw me a *Welcome Home* party. All the pussy I can handle."

The bartender poured me a shot and grabbed another six-pack of warm Michelobs, slamming the beers in front of Vern before moving back to the pool table. He checked the cue stick's chalk, applied more, blew on the tip.

Enrique's first song came on, fast rock and roll with too much enthusiasm for three guys drinking warm beers and whiskey in the middle of the day. He came back over, but didn't sit down, saying, "Got to go back to work, guys," and scratched at his tattoo, and because of his stubble, it made a noise like someone sweeping cement. He walked out.

"Tell me about the pruno," Vern said.

I couldn't tell him the truth: that I'd nurtured it, named it. That I didn't want to rip Madeline open and drink her blood. That I wanted to watch her grow up.

I slammed my shot and asked Vern for a warm one; he glared at me but handed over the beer.

"The pruno was delicious," I said, and even speaking those awful words sent a flicker, some sparks shooting through my good hand.

He snorted, fiddled with one of his sprawling eyebrows, rolling the hair into a point. "Pruno is a lot of things, but it's never delicious."

We nursed the next couple warm ones, not really talking too much. Finally, he said, "What are you doing here anyway? I thought we made the pruno because you were too broke to go to bars."

"This was an emergency."

He tapped me on my crooked arm. "That's an emergency."

I shrugged my shoulders.

"I'm a cheapskate," he said, "but even I'd fix that."

"I will."

"You should break it first."

"What?"

"Listen," he said, "you're going to have to pay more if you go with your arm like that. First, you'll pay for the doctors to break it. Then you'll pay for them to reset it."

"So what?"

"So break it yourself and save the money."

"That's crazy."

"I'll break it for you."

"Out of the question."

"Just remember who told you first," he said, holding his Michelob bottle up in my direction and taking a swig, making a crude *aahhh* noise when he finished swallowing his latest mouthful. "It would be my pleasure to break your arm."

LITTLE MAN

Letch asked for one good reason why I was taking so much shit from Sean Bourke. "Stand up for yourself," he said. "Fight fire with fire."

"What fire?" I said.

Letch told me to shut up and showed me a way to karate chop a guy in the Adam's apple. He showed me a way to twist someone's wrist behind their back so far it would break. He showed me his favorite move: how to lean in close to someone you were arguing with and say, "I didn't hear what you said," and when they started repeating their words, you head-butted them and cracked their nose.

"While they're standing there bleeding," Letch said, pretending to clutch a busted nose, "that's when you put your balls into stomping them mightily."

Sean had been beating up Skyler and me all year at school. Madeline had tried calling and telling the office about it, but they didn't do anything to stop him. Sean had moved to Phoenix from Wisconsin. He wasn't that tall, but he was fat and a lot stronger than us.

"After you do that," Letch said, laughing, "he'll offer to shine your shoes every day before class."

———

The next morning, Letch said, "I want you to do it today, Rhonda."

"What?"

"Get even with Sean. Do it before your mom comes back. That way the school will call me." He fuzzed my head. "Unless you like getting your ass kicked like a faggot." I shook my head *no*, and Letch said, "Make me proud, boy."

———

At lunch, all the kids were either playing tetherball or standing around talking. Sean was with one of his friends, over on the field. I'd told Skyler that I was going to kick Sean's ass. He said, "How are you going to do that?" and I said, "Letch taught me some tricks." Skyler told a bunch of kids what I was going to do. At lunch, all the kids were standing around waiting for me to make my move. No one thought I'd be able to do anything to Sean, but they were all excited to watch me get pummeled again. Skyler believed in me. He knew if anyone was mean enough to help us with Sean, it was Letch.

When I finally walked over to Sean, there were like fifty kids waiting for it.

I walked up to him, and he said, laughing, "I hear you're coming to kick my ass," and I said, "What?" and he made a fake scared face and said, "Are you going to beat me up?" pretending to bite his nails. "I can't hear you," I said, and he said, "What, are you deaf?" I took another step toward him. I was right in front of him. I said it again, "I can't hear you."

He leaned down a little and repeated himself, and I shoved every sliver of anger in my entire body up into my forehead. And right when Sean was in the middle of his sentence I thrust my forehead forward, crashing into his nose. He fell straight to the ground. He fell so fast there wasn't time to kick him in the balls like Letch had told me to.

Sean held his nose with both hands, screaming.

I started kicking him and I can't really tell you how many times I did it because once I started, he kept turning into different people: he was my mom so I kicked him; he was Letch so I kicked him; he was my real dad who I didn't know so I kicked him. I kept kicking until a teacher pulled me off and walked me to the principal's office.

———

Letch got to the school an hour later and met with me and the principal, who filled him in on what I'd done.

"I can't believe this," Letch said to her, shaking his head. "This will not go unpunished. I can promise you that."

The principal asked me to wait in the hallway so she and Letch could chat by themselves, and I left. I sat outside her office. The nurse's was across the hallway, and through the window I saw Sean walking with his mom. He held a bandage to his nose, and his head was tilted back.

I smiled.

Letch and the principal walked out, and he said, "I can't tell you how sorry I am about this. His mother and I will make sure this never happens again."

She nodded approvingly.

As soon as he and I were outside, he said, "Congratulations, little man."

He'd never called me *little man* before. I liked it.

"How'd you like it if I took you out for a steak?" he asked.

———

We went to a restaurant. He ordered two beers from the waitress and she giggled, saying, "He don't look twenty-one," and Letch said, "They're both for me, darling. I'm very thirsty," but when she brought the beers and had walked away, he slid a bottle to me, saying, "Here's to you busting noses, Rhonda."

We both drank.

It's hard for me to know how much to tell you about Letch because I don't want you to like him. But the truth is there were a lot of days where he was all right.

We drank our beers and ate steaks and everything was fun.

"Are you going to tell mom?" I said.

"Hell, no. She wouldn't understand."

"Where is she?"

Letch looked at me for a minute without saying anything. Then: "Do you miss your dad?"

"I don't remember him."

"At all?"

"Nothing."

"Jesus."

"Where's my mom always going?"

Letch finished his steak, his beer. "You'll have to ask her that one, Rhonda." He paid the bill, and right when we were leaving, he fuzzed my head and said, "I want you to know I'm real proud of you."

BLACK LUNGS

I lied to old lady Rhonda, after I'd gotten home from Vern saying he'd like to break my arm. I lied because how much more was I supposed to take that day? Handa told me about her big boy, Hector, and Vern offered to break my arm, but the worst part wasn't what he'd said, worst part was that it sounded like a good idea to me. I wanted him to break it. Smash the bone into glorious splinters. I wanted him to let me have it, the way Letch used to. So when I got to my apartment, and when old lady Rhonda came downstairs to watch "Wheel of Fortune," the first thing out of my mouth was, "Tomorrow's my birthday," and she said, "Really?" and I hated lying to her, really hated it, but I needed something good to happen, so I said, "Why would I lie?" and she laughed, which made me laugh, which made me feel a little better.

We sat on the burned couch, with our mugs of vodka. Commercials played on the TV. "Wheel of Fortune" would start any minute.

"This is so exciting," she said. "We'll have a little party. I'll bake a birthday cake."

"You don't need to do that. Let's just spend the night hanging out."

"What's on your wish list?"

"Nothing."

"Since you saved my couch and TV, I'll buy you anything you want."

"I don't want anything."

"Don't stomp on an old woman's heart, Crash Man. What would you like for your birthday?"

On the TV, Pat Sajak and Vanna White walked onto the stage. He was squinting and smiling; she was just smiling. The audience clapped.

"Let's play Wheel!" Pat Sajak said.

"I can have anything?" I said to old lady Rhonda.

"Name it."

"I've always wanted a tattoo."

"Do you already know what you'll get?"

"I've known for years."

She rubbed her hands together. She said, "I'll make an appointment. And invite anyone you want to the party. I'll bring my husband."

I drank my whole mug of vodka. There wasn't anyone I wanted to invite to the party, and I didn't want her husband there. I only wanted it to be the two of us. "Why would you bring him?"

"The more, the merrier."

"He lit your couch on fire."

"We've been married for thirty years. We have good phases and bad. You met him in a bad one."

"He shouldn't treat you like that."

She hugged me.

We hadn't been paying attention to "Wheel of Fortune" and someone had already solved the first puzzle.

"Don't worry about me," old lady Rhonda said. "I know how to deal with him."

I went into the kitchen and made another vodka rocks. I looked at the man shielding himself from the world with the pizza box on his face. "I don't want him at the party." I came back over and sat next to her.

"He's not so bad," she said and put her head on my shoulder. "Please… please let him come to the party."

How could I say no? The woman was throwing me a birthday party on a day that wasn't my birthday and offered to pay for a tattoo. I couldn't blackball her husband, even if I hated all the things he reminded me of: I needed my own pizza box to block out every niggling memory. "Fine."

"Maybe you'll even like him," she said, sounding like my mom prepping me to meet one of her new boyfriends. She'd introduced me to Letch in a bar, at a Mexican restaurant close to our house. She said, "This is my new friend," and she chewed the ice cubes in her wine spritzer, and he chewed the ice in his Bloody Maria. He nodded his head, slowly, and handed me some quarters. He said, "There's *Ms. Pac Man* by the entrance. Go play a few games on me."

"What do you say?" my mom said to me.

"Thanks."

"This is just the beginning," Letch said, fuzzing my hair.

"Beginning of what?"

"You'll see." He fuzzed my head again, and this time his watchband got snagged in one of my curls. I yelped. He smirked and said, "Sorry about that."

———

After old lady Rhonda had gone upstairs to cook her husband dinner, I lay in bed with Madeline. She smelled bad: mold in her bag, chunks of green floating on top of the orange liquid, like tiny lily pads.

I rested her on my chest.

I tucked her under my shirt so it looked like I was pregnant and put my hands on her, pretending to feel her kick.

I said, "I won't let anything happen to you."

I said, "You're safe."

I fell asleep like that, with Madeline slipped underneath my shirt.

———

About four a.m. I woke up from a nightmare. The same one I always had. I'm not ready to tell you about it yet. But I woke up and didn't want to go back to sleep. All I could think about was Vern. Vern cracking the bone in my arm, cracking it miraculously. In my fantasy, Karla was there, standing and watching, apologizing for all the awful things she'd said after I saved her life.

I dozed, in and out, and little-Rhonda said, "You still have that nightmare, huh?"

"A couple times a week."

"Is it still as scary?"

"Gets scarier every time."

He walked over and sat down on my mattress. The light on his helmet was on. He looked at Madeline, still under my shirt. I expected him to say something about her, but he never did. "Do you love the old lady?"

"Yeah."

"Does she love you?"

"I think so."

He turned his light off. "She's not our mom."

"She's better," I said.

———

When I opened my front door the next morning, old lady Rhonda wore a party hat, one of those cone-shaped jobs with the rubber band tucked under her chin. There were unicorns on it. Her gray hair was pulled back in another ponytail. She had a party favor in her mouth and blew it so it screamed; then she held it like a cigarette, while singing "Happy Birthday."

After her solo, she said, "Sorry to wake you up, but we need to get to the tattoo shop."

"Now?"

"You said you knew what you wanted so I made an appointment."

"I do. Thanks."

"Let's go," she said, blowing the party favor another time.

————

I took a shower and we walked up to Guerrero Street, avoiding Valencia. "They've got the whole neighborhood shaking like Baghdad today," old lady Rhonda said as cement trucks rumbled around, fixing spots that had been damaged on the sidewalk while jackhammers continued their clattering boom.

It was foggy out. A homeless man had hung shirts up on a chain-link fence, but because of the strong wind, they flopped around, a few falling. He asked if there was anything we wanted. Old lady Rhonda looked at the shirts. I looked down and was standing on another sidewalk stenciling, in silver spray paint: *You have less time than ever!*

I'd known for years that I wanted to get a Rorschach inkblot tattooed across my chest. I don't know why I kept putting it off. But I had the design. When they let me out of the hospital, I'd asked Angel-Hair to give me one of the inkblot cards. "Why?" he said, and I said, "Something to remember you by," but it wasn't just about him: it was also about my mom: this was one of the cards I used to see her face in when I gazed at it. Angel-Hair agreed to give me the card, saying, "Our secret, okay?"

I don't do it much anymore, but in those first years I was out, I used to stare at it all the time. Sometimes, I still saw my mom. Sometimes, Letch. Sometimes, though, I didn't see anything, just blackness, outer space, the womb, Damascus.

It was misting now, but because of the wind, the water was like spittle in our faces.

On the next block, a cab pulled over in front of us. A man leaned out the window and threw up. Old lady Rhonda winced, saying, "Happy birthday to you." She still wore the unicorn hat.

We walked into the tattoo shop, Permanent Evidence, and I

gave the inkblot design to the tattoo artist, telling him I wanted it from nipple to nipple. He had his whole body covered in work, at least as much of him as was showing. But I figured anyone who had a spider web tattoo on his face had probably run out of empty skin.

The guy gave old lady Rhonda a time estimate, saying he'd be done in about five hours, and she said to me, "I'll be back, birthday boy."

He and I didn't talk much. Just the buzz of the needle. The wiping of blood. I caught him looking at my crooked arm a few times and finally I said, "Motorcycle accident," and he nodded, saying, "Cool."

———

Old lady Rhonda was back right on time. She walked over to us, didn't say anything, staring at my Rorschach tattoo.

"Tell me what you see," I said.

"Black lungs," she said, leaning down and touching my chest. I still know the pattern her finger traced on my skin. "It's like you've chain-smoked for fifty years and I can see right through you."

———

Got a little jumpy after I went in my apartment and stripped naked and stood in the bathroom, looking at my tattoo. I felt weird that there wasn't anyone coming to my phony birthday party, not that I'd invited anyone, but still. Handa would be with Hector. Sure, old lady Rhonda would technically be there, but she'd really be with her husband. The tattoo needle in my good hand torqued to new velocities. Little-Rhonda appeared in the doorway.

"I like the tattoo," he said. "Angel-Hair would dig it."

"You think so?"

"No doubt."

"Hey," I said, wanting to buy my little chum a beer. "I'm going to Damascus to invite some people to my birthday party. Do you want to come?"

"Our birthday's not for a couple weeks."

"We're celebrating early."

"No thanks. Kids in bars. People get weird."

"Not mom," I said, but he still told me he'd pass.

———

I got to Damascus about three in the afternoon. The place was empty, except for Vern, sitting there with a warm one.

"Do you live here?" I asked him.

"Just the man I was thinking about."

"Me?"

"You and that arm. When we gonna break it?"

"It's my birthday."

"Happy fucking birthday."

"Thanks."

"When we gonna break that arm?"

"Do you want to come to my birthday party?"

He scowled and twirled one of his huge eyebrows. "Birthday party? What, are you ten years old?"

"Forget it," I said to Vern and asked the bartender for a shot of whiskey, who, in turn, asked to see my money first. I patted Vern on the back and said, "My friend here is buying."

Vern rolled his eyes. "Anything for the birthday boy. One for me, too." He shook his empty beer bottle: "Another dead soldier."

The front door opened and Enrique walked in. It turned out he worked at a metal shop around the corner called Meld, and he stopped in to Damascus a few times a day to drink a quick beer when the boss was gone. I looked at his *Gloria* tattoo and remembered mine.

"Check it out," I said to them and unbuttoned my shirt. My

tattoo was supposed to be covered in gauze for the first few hours, but I'd ripped it off. Both Vern and Enrique stared at it. "Tell me what you see."

"I see Bush drinking oil from a martini glass," Vern said.

"Really?" I asked. "You strike me as a republican."

"I may strike you, but I haven't been a republican since this buffoon botched everything."

"No shit?"

"I was a democrat 'til Bobby Kennedy died."

"So what are you now?"

"Morbidly disenchanted." With his hand, Vern imitated an airplane and crashed it into his warm one, knocking it over, suds foaming on the bar. "It's a demented world since 9/11, and old Vern wants no part of it." He picked up his empty bottle, banged it like a gavel. "Another dead soldier!"

The bartender came down, wiped up the mess, asked what had happened, but Vern just grinned at him. "May I have another ale, sir?" he said to the bartender, who begrudgingly obliged.

"What do you see, Enrique?" I said.

He rubbed his tattoo, saying, "I see Gloria, and she still hasn't forgiven me."

I buttoned my shirt back up.

"You guys want to come to my birthday party tonight?"

Vern stuck his little white tongue out again and made a farting noise.

"I'd love to," Enrique said.

"What?" Vern asked him, appalled.

"It's his birthday. Stop being such a prick."

"I am a prick."

"You're a prick who's going to a birthday party," Enrique said.

———

Around eight, everyone showed up to my apartment. First, Enrique and Vern, then old lady Rhonda and her husband, whose name was Lyle. She carried a chocolate cake with two candles jammed in its top: one said 3; the other said 0.

"Am I really turning thirty?" I said. "I still feel like such a child."

"That feeling never goes away," Lyle said, his teeth sticking out of his lips, like CD cases. "You get old and ugly, but you still feel like a baby on the inside."

I didn't want to talk to him. I took the cake from old lady Rhonda and carried it into the kitchen.

I introduced them to one another.

Vern had a six-pack of warm ones and two bottles of cheap champagne. He had a present, too, something wrapped in pages ripped from a porn magazine. He handed me the gift. "Let's open it after everyone goes home. It's kind of private."

"I didn't have time to wrap mine," Enrique said, as he handed me a bottle of whiskey, "but you seem to like this shit."

We shook hands.

Old lady Rhonda and Lyle had a present, too. She winked at me, "This is all we can afford."

I winked back and loved that we had an inside joke. "You shouldn't have."

"Open it," she said, and I tore the wrapping paper; it was a board game version of "Wheel of Fortune." "So you can practice, Crash Man."

We popped the champagne bottles and had a toast and proceeded to get drunk. Lyle eyeballed the burned couch and the TV. I could tell that they made him mad.

"How's the TV working out?" he said.

"Great."

"And the couch?"

"Better than nothing."

"Are you sure about that?" Vern said to me. "The thing stinks like an electrocuted monkey."

Everyone laughed, except Lyle, who asked, "What happened to your arm?"

"None of your business," I said.

"Boating accident," Vern said to Lyle. "Rhonda fell overboard. He was lucky to survive."

Old lady Rhonda could see things weren't going so well, so she said, "Lyle, will you help me cut the cake?" and they went into the kitchen.

Vern, Enrique, and I huddled on the burned couch.

"I don't like that guy," I said.

"Really? I hadn't noticed," Vern said, making another farting noise. "You don't camouflage your feelings too well."

"You want me to throw the guy out?" Enrique said.

"No. It's her husband. It'll be fine."

And then she came in carrying the cake and sang "Happy Birthday" again. Old lady Rhonda leaned down with the cake so I could blow out the candles without getting off of the couch. There was pride in her eyes, love in her eyes. "Make a wish," she said.

I thought about what I'd give her if it could be anything in the whole world and blew out the candles.

Old lady Rhonda screamed, "Hooray!"

Enrique clapped; Vern drank from a warm one; Lyle said, "Let's go home."

"You go," old lady Rhonda said. "I'll be up later."

"Let's go now."

"I'll be up soon."

"Now."

I stood up from the burned couch. "She doesn't want to go."

"I'm talking to my wife, not you."

"Boys, boys," Vern said. "Let's play nice before uncle Vern has to give both of you a marine-style talking to. Trust me, you don't want that."

"Are you coming?" Lyle said to old lady Rhonda, and she shook her head *no*. He left without saying another word.

"Temperamental fellow," Vern said.

"I'm sorry," old lady Rhonda said. "He's having a tough time." She grimaced, then looked at me and faked a smile. "Let's not ruin the party. Who wants more champagne?" and we drank what was left of the bubbly and moved on to whiskey.

Eventually, Enrique left. Eventually, old lady Rhonda kissed me good night and apologized for Lyle. I told her not to worry about it, but I was lying. It was well after three a.m., but Vern didn't want to leave until I opened his gift. We were on the burned couch. I opened the present, ripped right through the porn pages. Inside was a tire iron.

"Thanks," I said, "considering I don't own a car."

He shook his head, twirled a huge eyebrow.

"No seriously, thanks again," I said, "I think this will really come in handy."

"Jesus Christ."

"Really, I can wander around the neighborhood and help the less fortunate change their tires."

"It's not for a car, god damnit!" He flashed his little white tongue. "It's for your arm."

"What?"

"We'll use it to break your arm."

Me, Rhonda, drunk, confused. Wanting to buy a few minutes. "I've got to piss," I said to Vern and ran to the bathroom, trying to steady myself. I took off my shirt and stared at my tattoo, looked at all the things that lived in that one design, how a hundred people could see it and they'd all tell me something new, the freedom in that. I tried to think up some excuse to tell Vern, some reason I couldn't let him do it, but I wanted him to do it, but I didn't want him to do it, I had no idea what I wanted.

"Hey, I'm throwing up," I said to Vern. "Some other time."

"What?" I heard him walk over to the bathroom door. He knocked. "Let me in."

"I'm puking. We'll do this later."

"If you're so tanked you're puking, this is the perfect time to do it. Let me in."

"No."

He knocked again. "You won't feel any pain if you're that tanked."

"No."

"Let me in right now!"

"I can't."

"Open up, soldier!"

I wish I had a good reason for doing it. I wish there was something I could say that would make you understand why I opened the door. But I didn't have a good reason. I just did it. I opened the door and he stood there with the tire iron, hitting it against his open palm.

"Lay your arm on the countertop," he said.

I listened to him. I had to listen to him. Do you hear me?

I fell to my knees and lay my crooked arm on the counter.

"This is going to hurt worse than Jesus hurt," Vern said.

HOME-COOKED MEAL #2

One time my mom said she wasn't going to thaw dinner tonight, but cook, actually cook.

Letch put his hands to his cheeks and opened his mouth wide like he'd never been so astonished. "I'm sorry," he said. "I must have misunderstood what you said."

"Me, too," I said.

"I'm gonna cook dinner tonight."

"Are you sure that's a good idea?" I asked.

"Oh, Rhonda," Letch said, shaking his head, "she's finally trying to kill us."

———

It wasn't so bad. I mean, it wasn't good food. Most people probably wouldn't have eaten it. But my mom was home and she wasn't hitting the tcha-bliss too hard, and Letch was home, not hitting us too hard, and I was home, happy that we were all together.

She made chicken legs, cooked them in oil on the stovetop, and she served them with white rice that she'd pulled off the heat too early, making it feel like chewing little light bulbs.

That was all we got.

Letch looked at his plate and said, "No vegetables?" feigning shock again.

"I only know how to microwave vegetables," she said, "and I promised you boys no thawing tonight."

"What do you think, Rhonda?" Letch said. "Is she trying to poison us?"

I picked up my chicken leg and sniffed it. "Maybe."

"You first," Letch said to her, nudging me. "If she's alive in five minutes, you and me can dig in."

She took a bite of her leg, drank the rest of the tcha-bliss. She went and got another glass of wine before she'd finished chewing that first bite. When she came back to the table, she said, "I know you boys think you're pretty funny, but you better start eating before I get mad."

I still held my chicken leg up to my nose, but I didn't want to smell it again, seeing as how it stunk like the trunk of a car.

Letch said, "I'm not eating until I know you're not trying to kill us."

"Why would I want to kill you?"

"There's no reason. I'm just making sure."

My mom had another swig of tcha-bliss and said to me, "You don't think I'd poison you, do you, baby?"

I shook my head.

"Then eat, baby."

"Be careful, Rhonda. She's up to something."

"You guys," she said, "enough's enough."

I said to Letch, "I see what you mean," and set my chicken leg down on my plate.

"Baby, take a bite."

"Not yet," I said.

"The boy's only making sure it's safe."

She said, "This isn't funny." She said, "I cooked you boys dinner, now eat up."

"You look a little pale," Letch said to her. "How do you feel?"

"Eat your chicken!"

"All in due time."

"It's time."

"Can we trust her, Rhonda?"

"We better wait the five minutes," I said.

She finished her tcha-bliss, saying, "Why do I bother?" and she got up, knocking her chair over, and poured herself more tcha-bliss.

"We're just playing," Letch said.

"Then stop playing."

"I'm only verifying that your intentions were pure with this chicken."

"Enough already!"

"Rhonda, are you ready to dig in?" he said.

I picked up my chicken leg, held its scrawny shape up to my face. I could tell my mom was about to lose her temper, and I didn't want that, so I took a bite of the leg and said to her, "Mom, I really love this," but she stared at Letch and said, "Why do you want to ruin dinner?" and he said, "Relax, I'm only playing," and she said, "It's not funny," and he said, "We think it's funny," and I took another bite and while I was chewing I said to her, "Mom, this is wonderful chicken," and she said to Letch, "Are you going to eat it?" and he said, "Did you poison it?" and she said, "Stop saying that!" and I ate all of the meat off of my leg and took two huge spoonfuls of rice and shoved them in my mouth and tried to chew, but it was so big, my cheeks ballooning out, there was so much food I could barely speak, but I said, "This is so good you should make it again soon," and she said to Letch, "Why are you just sitting there?" and he said, "The five minutes aren't up yet," and she said, "I'm not trying to kill you," and he said, "We'll see," and he looked at me, saying, "Rhonda has taken his life into his own hands. What kind of mother are you?" and she stood up again, killed the rest of her tcha-bliss and said, "I'm going out," and I said, "Mom, look, look I've eaten all the chicken," as I stuck my spoon in the dune of rice, shoveling more into my mouth, and I said, "I'm still hungry. Will you make me some more chicken right now?" and she said to Letch, "I was trying tonight and you can't even give me that," and he said, "Stop it. I'm teasing. Watch," and he picked up his bony chicken leg and nibbled a little bite and said, "Satisfied?" and I shoved the last bit of crunchy rice into my mouth and said, "Can I have more chicken, please?" and my mom didn't even look at me, handing me her plate and saying to Letch, "Why can't you be nice?" and she finished her wine and poured herself more wine, and I ate all the chicken off of her bone, and crammed all the rice from her plate in my cheeks and I opened my mouth to say something, to tell her how amazing I thought her chicken was, but there was too much food and I choked a little, coughing and spitting rice all over the table. Neither of them looked at me. She said, "I'm gonna go out for a drink," and he said, "You never go out for just one drink," and I was coughing up rice but still trying to talk, I said, "This is the greatest chicken I've ever had in my life," and I coughed again, and she said to Letch, "What do you want from me?" and he said, "Learn how to take a joke," and she said, "As soon as you tell a funny one, I'll get it," and I coughed and said, "Man, this is superb chicken," and she said, "I'll be at the bar," and he said, "With who?" and I said, "Mom, would you mind making me more chicken?" and she said to him, "What do you care who I'm with?" and he said, "I care less and less every time," and she said, "This is the thanks I get for cooking," and I said, still chewing, still coughing, "Thanks so much for making the chicken, Mom," and Letch said, "Yeah, thanks," and she said, "Go to hell," and he said, "When did you lose your sense of humor?" and I was out of things to eat. My plate was clean. Her plate was clean. Letch's still had everything on it, except for his one tiny bite.

She got up, took her purse, and walked toward the door.

I said, "Where are you going?"

She said, "I'll see you later."

I said, "Later tonight?"

She said, "Maybe."

UGLY SMUDGES

I held Madeline close after Vern left. I was in bed, laying on my side, clutching her to my chest, my whole body heaving up congested hysterics. I lay there wondering why. Trying not to think about what I'd done. I didn't have a shirt on and I pinned Madeline to my tattoo and said, "Tell me what you see," but she didn't say anything. "Please, tell me," I said, pulling her in even tighter. Imagine me holding her tighter than I'd ever held anyone in my entire life. Imagine me, Rhonda, gripping Madeline's small body, like I was going to breastfeed her. And imagine how all that beauty got smeared into ugly smudges when I killed her. When I held her too tight and mauled her tiny frame, spilling everything out of her. Imagine the worst smell: mold and ketchup and orange juice that had been fermenting for weeks, suddenly pouring out of her, all over me, all over my sheets, blanket, mattress. Imagine that kind of guilt.

———

I'd gotten on my knees. I'd laid my arm on the countertop. I'd shut my eyes. I'd heard him say, "This is going to hurt worse than Jesus hurt," and I was ready for anything.

I wanted to open my eyes before he did it. I wanted to watch his face. Wanted to watch as he brought the tire iron down and shattered the bone. I wanted to know if there was pride or regret or anger or bliss. I wanted to know what Vern looked like because Letch never let me look up at him. So I looked at Vern. He hit the tire iron across his palm again. His smile. Letch's smile. They had fangs showing and I wanted the pain because I knew it, and it would make me happy, not happy exactly, but it would let me remember the things I've known, the things I've tolerated: even bad memories can make you happy because they're yours.

I was on my knees. "Do you want a blowjob?"

"What?"

I shimmied a little closer to him and said, "Blowjobs are when a girl puts your cock in her mouth."

"What the hell are you talking about?" He stopped hitting the tire iron across his palm and held it at his side.

"Do you want a blowjob?"

"Shut up."

I crawled closer. "Do you?"

"Shut the fuck up!"

"Do you?"

I crawled a little closer, but he edged back, holding the tire iron above my head like he was about to hit me with it. "You better shut the fuck up!"

"Do you want one?"

He kept the tire iron over my head and I waited for him to bring it down and split my skull, but he didn't swing it at me, dropping it on the floor.

I opened my mouth and said, "Please," and he said, "You're lucky I don't kill you."

I kept my mouth stretched open, like a screaming sidewinder.

"What the hell's the matter with you?" Vern asked.

I felt the skin in the corners of my mouth tear a little, tasting blood. I reached my arms out to touch his legs, but he shoved me away and stepped away and walked away.

I said, "Please don't go," but he'd already shut the door behind him.

———

I knew I should have showered the smell of Madeline off of me. But I couldn't. I was never going to see her again, and even though her smell was wretched, I didn't want to let her go; I needed to feel her for a little longer, even if the only way I could was to inhale her sour stink. My mattress, sheets, and only blanket were all soaked with her innards, so I bundled up in a couple of coats and slept on the floor next to their wet, tangled scent.

I hadn't had my eyes shut for ten seconds when little-Rhonda said, "What's that smell?" and sat down on the couch's arm.

"Not now," I said. "I've had an awful night."

"Let me make you a drink," he said, but all he did was go grab the whiskey, unscrew the cap, and hand me the bottle.

I took a sip.

"I'm assuming the party did not go well," he said.

I took another sip.

"I'm assuming your silence is a result of the party not going well."

I sipped again, too big this time, and got the feeling like I might lose it.

"I'm assuming your silence is the byproduct of testy communications during the course of the party."

"Not now."

"I'll change the subject. How was the old lady's husband? You bond?"

I swigged the whiskey again. "I hate him."

"Why?"

"She doesn't deserve it."

He grabbed the whiskey and took a sip, saying, "Deserves it? Who deserves it?"

——————

The next morning, I didn't know what to do with Madeline's dead body. I didn't want to pitch her in my trash. I put her in a paper bag and went out onto Valencia, still looking war torn, construction equipment everywhere. I figured I'd lay her to rest in the dumpster with the trapdoor. Yeah, it was still technically the garbage, but it was the garbage where little-Rhonda had taken me to the wonderful puddles.

But I didn't make it to the dumpster, because as I stood at a corner, I heard Handa say "Big Boy!" while she waved at me from across the street, across the battlefield of backhoes and forklifts. A crane lowered another new pipe into a trench.

My good hand held the bag, so I waved back at her with my bent arm.

She crossed the street toward me, through the chaos, past a lone worker shoveling dirt in another trench; all I could see of the person was the hardhat. It could have been little-Rhonda.

I tried not to panic, as Handa walked toward me, knowing I still stunk like Madeline's innards.

"Aren't you up early?" she said.

"Been helping a friend work in his attic. I'm sweaty. Sorry if I smell bad."

"Lucky for you, Valencia always stinks so your secret is safe. Can you believe how long the construction is taking?"

"I can't."

"It amazes me how long it takes them to fix things. I mean, what are they doing down there anyway?"

My good hand, still clutching Madeline, sputtered a low buzz, a noise like a didgeridoo. "Where's Hector?"

She scoffed. "Who cares?"

"What happened?"

"It's for the best." She smiled again. "I deserve someone who will treat me better. Someone nice, like you."

Me, Rhonda, she needed someone nice like me. Last time I'd seen her, I'd accidentally yelled, but she didn't seem to remember, and if she did, she didn't care. Unlike Karla, Handa must have been willing to give people the benefit of the doubt, even if they made a mistake. One of the backhoes backed up, making a beeping noise every second, and I thought it was my heart.

"Nice like me?" I said.

"Like you."

"You'd go out with someone like me?"

"Are you nice?"

I nodded.

She leaned her head onto my shoulder and said, "I'd go out with someone like you tomorrow night." I couldn't believe it. She'd never acted interested in me before. Or I hadn't noticed her flirting. "But you're right," she said, smiling, moving her head off of my shoulder, "you do smell bad."

"Sorry."

"I don't care. Just shower before our big date."

We came to the next corner, and I stared at the garbage can. I knew I should throw Madeline away, but it felt like a betrayal. My good hand turned up its electricity, jolts rollicking. I had to do it, knew I had to.

I put her in the garbage. I stood in front of another apartment building that was being converted into overpriced condos; I stood on another sidewalk-stenciling that said, *Who needs affordable housing anyway? Displacing the poor is better than cocaine!*

"You want to go out tomorrow night?" I asked Handa.

"I thought you'd never ask," she said.

———

I ran straight to old lady Rhonda's apartment to tell her about my date with Handa, but when she answered the door, she had a split lip and a bruise on her cheek.

"Don't say it," she said. Her gray hair was down, tousled, sticking every direction.

"He hit you?"

"We had a big fight. I was drunk. We were screaming."

"He hit you?"

"Don't worry about me, Crash Man. I can take care of myself."

I stood there, not knowing what to say next. I wanted to walk in old lady Rhonda's apartment and stay forever, protecting her.

Was I crying?

"It's okay, baby," she said, stepping out into the hallway and hugging me.

"I don't want him to hurt you anymore."

And I wanted to tell her about Vern and Madeline. I wanted to tell her about Letch. But most of all I wanted to stay in her arms.

"Please, baby," she said, and I said, "Why do they do it?" and she said, "Do what?" and I said, "Hit us."

We stood, swaying.

"You didn't come up here for this," she said. "What can I do for you?"

I honestly couldn't remember why I'd walked up there. Seeing her face all smashed had erased everything from my mind except protecting her. Finally, I remembered Handa and said, "I asked her."

"I thought she was out of town."

"Got back this morning."

"When are you going out?"

"Tomorrow night."

"Tomorrow! Congratulations. Let me make you some breakfast."

"Let me cook you breakfast," I said. "Since you've had such a rough time."

"You'd do that?"

I figured after making her throw me a phony birthday party, maybe I'd fake a Mother's Day for her. "Would you like breakfast in bed?"

Her eyes welled up. "Oh, Crash Man, you better not go giving an old woman a sense of hope."

TELL ME MORE

Right eye. I'd like to hear more about the house, he said. I didn't know what else to tell him. We'd been talking about the same things for days, months, years. I said, The house was evil. Evil, he asked. Cursed, I said. Left eye. Angel-Hair sat in front of me. His feet were flat on the floor. His left shoe had a huge scuff across its toe. Right shoe tapped twice. Tell me about your friend, he said. Skyler, I asked. Skyler, he said. His office smelled like tuna fish. Again. Still. Did Skyler see the house stretch, he said. It didn't move whenever anyone was in there besides me, my mom, and Letch. That's why the house is evil, because it keeps secrets, I said. Houses can't keep secrets, he said. Angel-Hair's eyes popped back and forth, focusing on my right eye then my left eye. His foot tapped a few more times. Letch would say, Is your boyfriend Sklyer coming over today. I'd say, He's not my boyfriend. He'd say, Why don't you ever bring any girls home. And Skyler didn't like coming to my house anyway. Letch made him nervous. And he knew my mom would take off for days on end. Letch would say, What time is your date with Skyler. He'd laugh and say, Are you the pitcher or the catcher. Right eye. Angel-Hair's foot still tapping. He said, So the house looked normal whenever Skyler was there. I knew what he meant. He meant the house wasn't stretched out, wasn't full of the desert. But Skyler never thought our house was normal. Skyler thought Letch was a creep. His eyes are like an eel's, Skyler said. And Letch would ask me, Have you and your boyfriend gone all the way yet. Who, I'd say. Don't be a smart ass, he'd say. Angel-Hair tapped his other foot, with the scuffed shoe. He looked down at it and frowned. Left eye. I said, The house looked normal when Skyler was there. Why, Angel-Hair said and licked his finger and leaned over and rubbed the scuff. It disappeared. He tapped that foot three times. He said, Houses aren't cursed or evil. I said, But all the bad stuff happened in there. He said, But the house didn't do the bad stuff. I didn't answer him. Wondering if every little kid who lived there would be shattered like me. Why don't you blame Letch, Angel-Hair said. Right eye. One time, Skyler was supposed to spend the night, but my mom and Letch finished a whole box of tcha-bliss and Letch was hollering and Skyler said his stomach hurt, called his mom, rode his bike home. I looked at Angel-Hair's shoe again. The scuff was drying and coming back. Angel-Hair said, I asked why you don't blame Letch. Left eye. My mom had this weird way of talking after she'd drank a lot of tcha-bliss, her words stretching into humungous vowels. Another time, Skyler and I played in my room, and Letch came in and said, What are you up to in here, ladies. We didn't say anything. He said, Ladies, do you need some birth control pills. What's birth control pills, I said. Skyler shrugged his shoulders. Letch said, Faggots. Angel-Hair's shoe without the scuff tapped five times. Right eye. Tell me why you don't blame Letch, Angel-Hair asked. How do you know I don't blame Letch, I said. You always talk about the house, he said. I blame both of them, I said. You can't blame the house, he said. But I could. I could blame anything. Anyone. I wasn't through with that house yet and some day I'd make sure no other kid got shattered in there. Hey, ladies, Letch said. What time is the wet T-shirt contest, he asked. I have to go, Skyler said. Don't go, I said. So long, farewell, Letch said to him. What if someone had hidden a can of tuna fish in Angel-Hair's office days, months, years earlier, and the doctor didn't smell it because he was used to it, and why was it called tuna fish anyway. Why wasn't it just called tuna. There were lots of fish. Salmon, trout, halibut, sturgeon. No one said trout fish. Or sturgeon fish. Left eye. He licked his finger again, leaned down, rubbed the scuff. Why can't I blame the house, I said. Do you know what blame is, he said. Blame is placing responsibility on someone, he said. Can't you blame something, I said. No, he said. If I got struck by lightning, I said, can't I blame it. Blame the lightning, he asked. I nodded. Both of his feet tapped twice. No, he said. But I knew I could. I could blame anything. Another time, Letch said, Skyler, you and Rhonda make a lovely couple. Skyler dropped his eyes to the floor, didn't say anything. I dropped my eyes to the floor, too. I said, Where's mom. Letch said, Search me. Angel-Hair said, Blame was created by humans, for humans. Blame only has power if the person knows what he or she did was wrong. Right eye. I had him. I knew that the house knew what it did was wrong. That was the only reason it looked normal whenever Skyler came over or one of Letch's drinking buddies was there. One time Letch and his friend were in the kitchen and I walked in and they stared at me so I said, Hey, ladies, who's pitching and who's catching. Letch's friend laughed and said, Kid's got a big mouth. Letch said, You better get out of here, Rhonda. The house only looked normal because his friend was there, but I knew as soon as he left, things would warp again.

THE LEVERS OF FATE

I was with Angel-Hair during high school, and there weren't any proms in there. But I'd seen them on TV, so I knew this was as close as I'd ever come: old lady Rhonda fussing over me, getting me ready for my big date with Handa.

She also gave me $100.

"I can't take this," I said, and she said, "Oh, please," and I said, "No, seriously," and she said, "Then pay me back once you start working again."

And I'd been thinking about work. I'd run into an old co-worker who told me the place he was at needed line cooks. "The food is shit," he'd said, "but it's all the beer you can drink after your shift." It wasn't how I'd dreamed it: I'd fantasized about moving to San Francisco and someday cooking at my own restaurant, featuring Meat Trees, but this would have to do.

I took a shower to wash Madeline's scent off of me. Someone in the building must have spent the whole day running hot water because mine was freezing. I stood in the stream, goose bumps raised on my skin, even under my Rorschach tattoo. I rubbed my hand over it, feeling it like Braille, wondering what a blind person would see running their fingers across its topography.

———

Once I was out of the shower, I smelled my hands, my arms, my shoulders, trying to inhale the slightest trace of Madeline, but she was totally gone. I put on clean clothes, shoved my curls around until they looked less like Vern's eyebrows, which wasn't easy since my hair was thick as asbestos.

The last thing that happened before I left for the restaurant was old lady Rhonda holding up a camera and screaming, "Say cheese!" and snapping a picture. She smiled and said, "That one's going on my fridge," which made me think about the pizza-box-picture on mine and I was happy.

———

"Are you ready for this?" Handa asked, motioning her arms down her body like she was the grand prize on "Wheel of Fortune," performing a slow pirouette.

"I think so," I said, excited. Nervous.

She looked fantastic: pants hugging the shape of her legs, an inch of skin showing above them, showing those divine black hairs, a wreathe around her bellybutton. Her shirt stretched like a lucky water balloon, holding all of her in there.

We walked to a small Italian place on Valencia, between 23nd and 24th. There were only four tables in the dining room. The owner was the waiter. And the cook. He sat us in the window. We were the only people in the place. He asked us what we'd like to drink.

"Do you like red wine?" I said to Handa, and she nodded, so I said to the owner, "Bring your favorite bottle of red, please," but as soon as he walked away, I told her I needed to use the bathroom and I followed the owner, whispering, "When I said 'bring your favorite,' I meant 'bring your cheapest.'"

"Sparing no expense, huh?"

I didn't have time to care what he thought.

I went back to the table.

We shared an antipasti plate and polished off the wine, while I listened to her talk about her life. And it was weird because I tried, I really tried to listen to what she was saying, but I couldn't stop thinking about what I'd say if she asked about my life, which made my maraca toss and turn, made me feel far away from her, like she was an astronomer looking at me through a telescope.

"Do you like working with your father?" I said.

"No."

"What's wrong with it?"

"He drives me pretty nuts. Not that I can blame that all on him." She stared in my eyes. "I can go a little crazy every now and then."

"Join the club."

"I started the club!"

"But seriously, what drives you nuts about working with your dad?"

"He wants me to get married. Have twenty-five Muslim babies. Do what my husband says."

We flagged down the owner. He brought us a new bottle and opened it. We ordered entrees. We were still the only people in the restaurant.

"What do you want?" I said.

"To have my own life before I'm a mother. To really accomplish something. To get out of that liquor store and do something surprising. Something no one ever thought I was capable of doing." She smiled. "Maybe I'll win a Nobel Prize."

"I believe it."

Handa bit her lip and looked at the ceiling. I'd never noticed before, but there was a small scar on her forehead, in the shape of a wasp. "I don't expect to save the world," she said, "but I'd like people to know that I was in it."

The owner refilled our wine glasses.

"What about your life?" she asked me.

My maraca shook faster. "What about it?"

"Tell me everything."

I drank all of my wine in a big sip, and she stared at me. "I'm not sure what to say. I guess I'd change it all."

"Everything?"

"I'd start all over. New parents. New life. Possibilities."

"You don't feel like you have possibilities?"

"Not really."

"How sad!"

"Is it sad? I don't know. I like cooking. Some days that's enough."

"And you take pictures."

"And I take pictures."

"How long have you lived in San Francisco?"

"About ten years. Since I was twenty." Once the words were out of my mouth, I couldn't believe I'd been here that long. It felt like ten months, like ten tiny months ago I'd fled Phoenix. Angel-Hair had arranged for me to get a job after I got out of the hospital, but six, ten, fifteen months later, everything there reminded me of everything I'd lost, and I needed to escape that emptiness. Even emptiness can suffocate you.

"What brought you here?"

"I was working at a drugstore in Phoenix. My boss knew I liked to cook and he had a buddy in SF who owned a restaurant. He phoned in a favor. I moved here, started peeling garlic and potatoes, worked my way up."

"Is that what you do for a living?" She finished her wine. I split the rest of the bottle in our glasses.

"When my arm isn't broken, yes."

The owner brought our entrees, grated fresh cheese on our pastas.

"I want you to cook me dinner. Do you have a secret recipe?"

I nodded. "Meat Trees."

She laughed and said, "What are Meat Trees?"

Hearing her laugh was like she'd taken everything awful and everything I'd squandered and turned it into an ant, one tiny ant that I could barely see, something so small that it couldn't hurt me anymore, and if I held the ant, if I placed it on my skin, I'd feel its tiny weak legs walking all over me and I'd know that everything was going to be all right.

"You'll see. Would you like to take a walk after dinner?"

———

It was really cold, but we stuck with the plan, combing the streets of the Mission. We got big cups of coffee at Muddy Waters, strolling down Valencia, its unpaved chaos, its sleeping monsters still lined the side of the road. We passed an Irish bar that had "With or Without You" playing on the jukebox. I told Handa that you could go into any Irish bar in San Francisco and within fifteen minutes, a U2 song would come on.

"Why?" she said.

"Name another Irish rock band."

She didn't even have to think about it. "Flogging Molly."

"I think they're Americans."

"No, Irish."

"Irish-Americans?"

"Maybe," she said, "but I doubt it."

"My point stands: fifteen minutes in any Irish bar in SF and U2 will play."

We peered through the bar's foggy window. Not a woman in the place. Skinny and pale men singing along with Bono, serenading imaginary lovers.

"Will you play a game with me, Big Boy?"

"Sure."

"I'll show you something I love. And you show me something you love."

I knew right away that I wanted to show her my Rorschach tattoo; she'd stare at it and suddenly she'd see something astonishing. "Can I go first?" I said. "I've got a good one. We need to go to my apartment."

"Ooooh. Trying to take me home already?"

We started walking toward my apartment, but we only took a couple steps.

Then I saw where we were.

Where we were standing.

What was right next to us.

I froze.

This couldn't be a coincidence. No way. I felt the levers of fate steering me in a certain direction.

Look at the facts: Handa and I strolled down Valencia, sipping coffees, talking, and out of nowhere she suggested that we share something that we loved with each other, and now we were in the one place in the entire world where I could really share something that I loved.

Me, Rhonda, her, Handa…

…right in front of the taqueria…

…the taqueria with the dumpster…

…the dumpster with the trapdoor…

And right then I knew that I was supposed to take her down with me, supposed to show her the secret passageway into the sewer system and help her climb down the humungous ladder and help her find her way through all those dark tunnels and show her the puddles, show her that there was one way left for me to see my mom.

"Are you all right?" Handa said.

I still hadn't taken a step.

"Big Boy, is something wrong?"

"Let's go back there," I said, motioning to the alley behind the taqueria.

There were no streetlights down the alley. Just darkness. Just secrets.

"Why?" she said, and I said, "Trust me."

"Too spooky," she said, and I said, "It's back there," and she said, "What is?"

"What I love," I said, "is back there," and I knew she was

scared, but there was no reason to be scared, I wanted to tell her that this was the kind of thing you did when you were falling in love, when your names rhymed, when you'd just had a magnificent dinner together. I wanted to tell her that I understood she was uneasy and apprehensive, but I'd never let anything happen to her, because she made me happy and I'd never been happy, and we could be happy for the rest of our lives. She was safe and loved, and I was safe and loved, and nobody was ever going to hurt us. I wanted to tell her that maybe people could be happy, maybe people could sculpt happiness out of all their shapeless disasters. I'd tell her that we could build it, and we wouldn't have to do anything except breathe, because everything else would already be in place and everything would already be beautiful and we'd be beautiful, and the only thing we'd ever have to worry about again is breathing, that was it.

"Is there another way we can go?" she said. "This is spooky."

"You're safe," I said and took her wrist with my good hand and guided her. The alley had the smell of boiled chicken and onions, and Handa wasn't walking fast. I practically dragged her. Forced her. But I knew in the end this would all be worth it. All she needed to do was see where we were going, where we were going to end up, and she'd trust me forever.

"Let's go back," she said.

"We're almost there."

"You're hurting my wrist."

I let go of it and said I was sorry.

She rubbed the spot where my hand had been.

I stopped in front of the dumpster and patted its metal side. "This is it."

"You love this?"

"I love this."

"You love a dumpster?"

"It's not just a dumpster."

"Can we leave?"

"Trust me."

"Please?"

"You won't believe this."

"I'd like to leave."

"Just give me a second."

"Can we please leave?"

"Hold on," I said, knowing there was nothing I could say to make her understand; she had to see with her own eyes, had to see the trapdoor and the huge ladder snaking down into the darkness. She needed to experience it all for herself and then she'd understand.

I threw the dumpster's lid open and was trampled by its humid breath, yawns of awful odors, all those wasted meats – steak and pork and chicken – rotting and steaming in the dumpster's stomach, and lucky for me, it was only half-full this time so I jumped in and burrowed through the swampy textures, but it was slow going because of my crooked arm, and Handa said, "Big Boy, please, stop!" and I said, "Just wait one second," and she said, "I'm leaving," and I said, "I know this seems weird, but trust me."

I continued my excavation, tunneling deeper, throwing handfuls of old napkins and Styrofoam boxes and clumps of rice into the alley, and she said again, "Please stop!" but my fingernails were already scratching against the dumpster's metal bottom, I didn't even throw the rest of the trash out, scooting it into the corners. I told Handa, "I can't wait for you to see this," and she said, "Stop, please," but I was so close, launching the last bits of trash out of my way, and the door should be right here. The door should have been right here. But it wasn't. I told myself not to be scared, to stay calm. The garbage that I'd only pushed aside before, now I heaved every single thing out of the dumpster, because this was all some mistake, some misunderstanding, I knew there was a trapdoor, I'd already squeezed through it and I was going to do it again, we were going to do it together, Handa and Rhonda. We'd squeeze through, and this was the beginning of a happy life together.

———

I couldn't bring myself to go to Damascus because I didn't want to see Vern and I obviously couldn't go to Handa's store. Lucky for me, there were entire constellations of liquor stores in the Mission; I bought bourbon and brought it back to my apartment, plopped down on the burned couch. Drinking. Staring at the bend in my arm. Inflating with humiliation, swelling like Madeline had done. Waiting for the warp in my arm to speed up, for my arm to suddenly wrap around my neck like a boa constrictor and put me out of my misery. Thinking about my mom, leaving. How everyone leaves, and no one cares, and why didn't she visit me when I was in the hospital, and why didn't she try to reach me after I got out, why hasn't she called me to say I know you had depersonalization and I'm sure you regret what you did, but I should have done a better job protecting you and the past is the past and let's try and be a family?

And thinking about Handa, too, as she ran down the alley, away from me and the magic dumpster, as I stood in it, trash thrown everywhere, thinking about her telling me to stay away from her and never come in the store again, I mean NEVER, EVER, or I'll call the police, I NEVER WANT TO SEE YOU AGAIN!

I stormed into the kitchen and took the picture of the homeless man and his pizza box off the fridge, ripped it up, shoved it into my mouth, washed it down with a huge swig of bourbon. My eyes welling up. I didn't need that picture. Things couldn't be worse. I'd been wrong. Been wrong this whole time. Things were awful and life was awful and there was no way all this sadness would ever be conquered by anything else. Life was just a collection of sadness, an acceptance of sadness, its prowess caging us all in regret.

Then I heard purring coming from inside the burned couch. I jumped up. Stood in front of it. Something slithered around under the couch's charred fabric, like a burst of liquid navigating a vein. I leaned over and pushed on it, expected it to buckle under the pressure from my finger, but it was hard, felt strong. The purring got louder. I knew the noise. It was a sidewinder. One of my friends. I went to the kitchen for a knife and cut a deep gash in the arm of the couch, a gash much deeper than the fire's damage, and a sidewinder fell out of the couch and onto the floor. It coiled and purred and I got down on the floor, stuck my face right up to it. Felt the calming flit of that cold tongue. That loving tongue. Touching me in rhythmic rushes, fast lashings. My old friend, my protector, we'd spent so much time together. I'd hide and you'd watch out for me, wouldn't let anyone hurt me.

But the snake lodged its fangs in my neck. Latched on and wouldn't let go. Me, Rhonda, betrayed again. I rolled around on the floor. Trying to rip it off but it was hopeless. There was nothing I could do. I yanked on the shaft of its body, but it wouldn't let go. I could feel the venom shooting from the fangs. Could feel it blasting through me at mach speeds. It was like all that poison ran straight to my brain. Because suddenly I knew what I was supposed to do. Suddenly I knew what was supposed to happen. I knew that there was a way to make everything in my life all right again. Nothing was going to get better until I took care of the past. Locked it away so it couldn't keep coming back from the dead.

The snake shot one more massive blast of venom into my neck; I stopped moving and my hands buzzed, even my mannequin hand. The snake wound up the couch's leg and wiggled back into its decimated guts; I lay on the floor and listened to every whisper that came to me from the poison, those supple suggestions, as the venom outlined the plan.

―――――

When I woke up, my head rested in little-Rhonda's lap. The light on his helmet was off. He stroked my hair.

"Am I dead?" I asked.

"What did it tell you to do?"

"We have to go to Phoenix."

"Why?"

"To burn down our house."

PSYCHIC KID

Before Letch lived with us, my mom used to take me on her drinking expeditions. She didn't like to pay for cocktails or babysitters. We'd walk into one of our regular bars, and some guy would say, "Hey, look, it's the psychic kid." Everyone would smile at me and slap my shoulders as we walked deep into the joint. Mom would help me onto a stool, and the bartender would put a 7UP with a handful of old cherries in front of me. "It's on the house, kind sir," he'd say, and my mom would lean across the bar and kiss him on the cheek, ordering herself a fuzzy navel. Blended. Nice and thick.

Tonight, the bartender's name was Jerry, and his beard was black, but on one side of his face, he had a patch of gray whiskers, like someone had soaked a paintbrush and smacked him across the cheek with it.

"I can beat the psychic kid tonight," he said, winking at my mom.

Since she didn't like to pay her bar tab, my mom made all these drunks believe I was psychic. Really, I was just honed. We'd spent hours practicing the scam. She'd make me do it over and over again, saying, *I need you, baby. We don't have much money so we have to improvise.*

I never thought to ask where she learned this trick. I did what she told me to.

Mom would take a square cocktail napkin and lay it on the bar and put a quarter on each of its corners. I was to shut my eyes and hold my hand over them, so there was no way I could peek.

Then the newest contestant would point at one of the quarters, and it was my job to KNOW which quarter they picked. If I was right, they had to buy my mom a drink.

And I was always right. I'd uncover my eyes and wave my hand over the napkin all slow, pretending to feel the quarters' auras, really milking the moment because all the people around us would be paying attention to me, and I can't tell you how good it felt, even now just thinking about it, I remember those nights being warm. Once, one of my uncles in that alcoholic family had come up to me after I'd dazzled him by picking the right quarter; he got down onto a knee, onto my level, and looked me in the eye: "I used to be just like you," smiling, "but now I'm a disaster."

Sometimes while I'd be surrounded by all of them, I'd even say, "Abracadabra!" I'd say it because it made everyone howl, big toothy grins showing over the lips of their cocktail glasses.

Not that I needed any magic. I always picked the right coin. Remember this was white trash sleight-of-hand. My mom had a cocktail napkin under her drink, too, so when the latest contestant selected a certain quarter, my mom would take a sip of her blended – nice and thick – fuzzy navel and she'd set it back down on the corner of her drink's napkin that corresponded to the corner that the person had just picked on the other napkin. All I had to do was give a sneaky glance at my mom's drink, and I always knew which corner was the winner.

That night, though, I was tired of playing the psychic kid. We'd been out drinking four nights straight and I just wanted to go home.

"What's your wager?" my mom said to Jerry.

"I'll bet you three cocktails I can beat the psychic kid," he said, patting my shoulder. "This little champion."

I should tell you, too, that my mom didn't have any money. Why would she bother to bring any along? I never lost.

The bar's crowd closed in around me, about twenty people,

mostly gray hairs, except for my mom. She set up the scam: square cocktail napkin, quarters on its corners.

She told me to lay my head on the bar, which was kind of sticky on my forehead and smelled like black licorice. She told me not to cheat.

While my head was down, Jerry pointed to one of the quarters.

While my head was down, I decided that I didn't feel like being a psychic kid tonight and since I knew my mom didn't have any money, I figured we would have to go home if I got it wrong.

While my head was down, I decided that definitely, definitely I would get it wrong.

I raised my head and didn't look over at her cocktail napkin. I made sure she noticed, too, that I wasn't looking over there. I kept my neck craned up, eyes closed, pretended I was contacting the spirits that were going to help me pick the right quarter.

"Abracadabra!" I said, and right on cue, the entire clog of people fixed around us released their jaded laughs. I did a few more waves of the hand and said, "The spirits have spoken and I know which one it is."

I pointed at a quarter.

Suddenly there wasn't any talking or laughing. All the airborne syllables died. All the bar's noises were pulled into a vacuum and held hostage.

"This the one?" I asked.

"No," Jerry said.

The people, my extended family, slinked and limped away from me.

My mom yanked me off the stool before I'd even had a chance to eat all the old cherries bobbing in my 7UP. She told Jerry we'd be right back. She heaved me through the bar's front door and as soon as we were in the parking lot, she said, "You've got some nerve."

"It was a mistake," I said.

"Like hell," she said. "What's wrong with you?"

"There's nothing wrong with me."

"Why did you do it?"

A cockroach walked between us on the pavement and I stepped on it.

I could tell she wanted to scream, that she wanted to get really heated about this, but something seemed to erode her hostility. The look in her eyes wilted from anger to sadness. She sank her hand in her purse and fumbled for her keys, pulling them out, accidentally dropping them in the mucus of squashed roach.

"Hopeless," she said, bending over to grab them and smearing the crushed bug on her skirt. She turned and walked to the car without looking at me. "Everything is hopeless."

EL PASADO

Little-Rhonda and I rented a Dodge Neon and sped south on I-5. I kept seeing these odd black shapes scattered on the side of the road that looked like dead seals, but they were only blown tires.

Music yelled on the speakers. Rock and roll.

I hadn't stopped smoking since we started driving.

Little-Rhonda rubbed the dashboard and said, "Is this the best you could do?"

"It's not so bad."

"We couldn't have done much worse."

"It's got four wheels," I said. "There's an engine."

"You sure about that?"

I turned the music up even louder, drowning him out. There were vicious guitars and a female singer spreading rumors about a man who'd broken her heart and blackened her eye and disappeared without a single word.

"Are you okay?" little-Rhonda yelled.

"I'm fine."

Before we'd left, I'd run upstairs and given old lady Rhonda the keys to my apartment, and an invitation to come down to my place any time she felt like it, told her to swig cheap vodka and eat all the cheese sandwiches she could handle, that I had to go to Phoenix for a couple days, but please, enjoy the couch and TV, feel free to crash at my place if he's had too much to drink and seems mean, and I'd be back soon to watch "Wheel of Fortune" with her every night.

———

There hadn't been time before we'd left to change my clothes, so there were bits of food and dumpster-snot all over me, which I wouldn't have even noticed, but the next thing I knew, little-Rhonda snatched something off my shirt and said, "Yum. Chicken!" and he stuffed it in his mouth like we were gorillas and he was eating tics from my fur.

———

Later, a snake slithered up and sat on little-Rhonda's shoulder. It purred. Just seeing the sidewinder reminded me of being bitten. Of the feeling of betrayal as the fangs broke my skin and spilled their poison. The crushing feeling of betrayal when someone you trusted opened its mouth and bared its brutal teeth.

"Why'd that sidewinder bite me?" I asked.

"Tough love," he said.

———

As the sun came up and we were somewhere in the Central Valley, a crop-duster flew over the fraying heads of corn stalks. The plane dropped low, right over the corn, and released a yellowy film. I stopped watching the road, couldn't take my eyes off the crop-duster. I didn't know how long it was until I looked back at the road, and I wouldn't have cared if the highway curved and the Neon ended up in a ditch, all smashed up. That was how perfect it was, watching the plane scribble the sky with a jaundiced dust that drifted down to the corn, like toxic confetti.

———

We drove into Phoenix, trying to find our way back home. The entire desert had been obliterated. Paved. Developed. There weren't even cacti, especially the huge Saguaros that I used to see everywhere, lining the roads anymore. All cut down, all murdered.

I didn't recognize any landmarks, but I remembered all the major streets. I knew we stayed on Shea Boulevard, and the tiny neighborhood I used to live in would be on the right-hand side.

My good hand jumped to microwave-popcorn-mode, kernels colliding.

Little-Rhonda and I sped through mid-day traffic.

"What's going to happen?" little-Rhonda said.

I tried to say something confident, so he knew I'd take care of this, and that there was nothing to worry about. "After it's burned, we'll roast marshmallows in its ashes."

"We don't even like marshmallows," he said.

"That's not the point."

"When was the last time you even had a marshmallow?"

"They're metaphorical marshmallows."

"What's the metaphor?"

"Shut up," I said.

———

I wondered what would happen if there were people in the house when I got there. Hopefully the house would be empty. Kids at school. Parents at work. All I'd have to do is break a window and climb in and walk around the house with a book of matches, lighting curtains, carpet, clothes. I'd stand there as the fire really started cooking, stand there to make sure that it wouldn't be saved by eager firefighters, I'd search the garage for flammable chemicals, cleaning products, whatever I could find to seduce the blaze into bulging, bloating flames slipping into the house's frame, burning the insulation in the attic, burning the walls that kept Letch's secrets, and I won't let it happen again. I'd flip the gas knobs on the stove to high, drench the coats in the hall closet in hairspray before holding a match to their sleeves. The smell of dying trees. Glass exploding. I'd smile and cough and stagger and watch the house crumble, its support beams withering to sticks and caving in from the weight, wood crashing to the flaming carpet, the house dying: there would never be another atrocity within these walls, the sinister way the walls concealed all that malice.

———

But what if there were people in the house? What if the mom didn't work or the dad didn't work or the kids were home, swarms of chicken pox pocking their skin? What if they sat in front of the TV, the kids slurping homemade soup, trying not to scratch the pox, don't scratch, if you do, they'll never heal, they'll just scar, you don't want to spend the rest of your lives walking around covered in scars, do you?

I'd have to find a peaceful way to lure them out of the house. Because I was not there to hurt anyone. Just the opposite. I was there to protect people.

I'd tell them I work for the city of Phoenix and that there was a gas leak on the block and that they needed to vacate the premises immediately, for their own protection. I'd smile and tell them there isn't anything to worry about, and I'd lead them to the street before I ran inside and lit everything on fire that would catch. Then I'd run out front and try to console them as they watched the spirits of their worldly possessions take off to the sky in billowy shapes, the cremains scattering in an Arizona wind. I'd console them, give them a shoulder to cry on. I'd say, "I know what it's like to lose everything."

———

Little-Rhonda and I should be there any minute.

The name of our street was El Pasado.

That was the name of the street where the house was.

Our house was actually the first one on El Pasado.

Our house was immediately on the left-hand side.

The address was 7876.

Our house used to be light brown.

It might still be light brown.

But another family might have painted it a different color.

That family may have little kids, and they were the reason I was doing this. The house used to have black pebbles in the front yard.

It used to be my job to rake those pebbles.

Letch used to water the pebbles.

I never knew why he watered the pebbles.

What would water do for pebbles?

El Pasado could be any of the next few blocks.

I drove a little slower.

I braked before each possible turn.

I squinted to read the street signs.

I didn't slow down at the next intersection, though, because a huge shopping center took up the whole side of the street. The sprawling store was painted orange. It was a huge Home Depot. I shook my head in disgust because of its hulking ugliness, and as we passed the street sign, little-Rhonda said, "That was it," and I said, "What?" and he said, "You missed it."

I looked over at the shopping center as we sped by. "Missed what?"

"El Pasado."

"It couldn't be."

"That was it."

"Are you sure?" I asked and moved the car across the three lanes of traffic so I could do a U-turn and find out if little-Rhonda was right. He hadn't steered me in the wrong direction yet, and if he was right, my worst fear was confirmed: our little house didn't have a backyard anymore, no access to the desert, but sat there dwarfed in Home Depot's orange shadow.

I backtracked, then turned onto El Pasado, pulled the car over. I didn't look to the left-hand side of the street yet. Not ready to see 7876 El Pasado.

Little-Rhonda said, "Show time, baby" – giving a loud round of applause – "this is the moment we've been waiting for."

I smiled at him. I wanted to say something to let him know I appreciated him being with me. I remembered how comforting it felt when old lady Rhonda had said these simple words so I repeated them now: "My little Crash Man."

"What?"

"Forget it."

I was finally ready to eye the street, to see my stretching house. I looked over at it. To that lair of haunting agony. I looked over to my house, to where my house should be. I looked over to where the house was supposed to be. But it wasn't there. 7876 El Pasado wasn't there.

What I saw instead of 7876 El Pasado was one of Home Depot's massive orange walls.

"Where is it?" little-Rhonda said.

I didn't answer him. Lost in all that orange. Thinking about a gigantic bag of pruno.

"Where is it?" he said again.

"It's gone."

"Gone?"

"Everything's gone," I said, looking up the street. There used to be ten other houses on El Pasado, too, but they'd all been leveled, all demolished, as if they'd never existed.

The last thing I did was look to the corner, to where I used to catch the bus to school, but now it was a corral for Home Depot's shopping carts.

TELL ME MORE

Right eye. It was a different day or month or year, but we were
still talking about Letch. About the house. About the house I
hated, and I kept saying to Angel-Hair that someone should
burn it down. He asked me why I blamed the house. He said,
Didn't bad things happen outside of the house. No, I said.
Only in the house, I said. Angel-Hair had rolled the sleeves
on his shirt up to his elbows. His wrists, so weak, so brittle.
He could probably put a watch on too tight and fracture the
bone. Left eye. Sometimes good things happened outside the
house, I said. Like what, he said. The amnesty bench, I said.
The hospital's air conditioning didn't work, and it was summer.
Every room smelled like onions. An amnesty bench was where
I could say anything to Letch and he wouldn't hit me, I said. I
had one minute to say anything I wanted and there wouldn't be
any consequences. Why would he do that, Angel-Hair asked.
His father had done it to him. In Detroit. His father was a
prison guard and told Letch, Even the inmates need to vent.
With his sleeves rolled up to the elbows, I couldn't believe how
skinny Angel-Hair's wrists were. If he clapped, the bones would
splinter. If he sneezed really hard in his hand, he'd lose a few
fingers. Right eye. Tell me more, he said. We didn't have a bench
in our backyard. Letch took me to the grocery store. There was
a wooden bench out front. An awning to protect people from
the Arizona sun, but the awning had been tattered, destroyed. I
sat down and the bench burned the backs of my thighs. Don't

be a faggot, Letch said. What did you say to him, Angel-Hair asked. You've got sixty seconds, Letch said and looked at his watch. Go, he said. We sat next to each other. Letch was all sweaty. Must have been a hundred-fifteen degrees that day. He smoked, too, big pulls on his hand-rolled cigarettes. His body twisted to the side to look me in the eyes. Talk, Rhonda, he said. No second chances, he said. Angel-Hair's shirt was light blue. He sat with his hands clasped behind the back of his head and sweat had tie-dyed the armpits in circular stains. I don't know what to say, I told Letch. Hurry up, he said. Just tell me what you think of me, he said. I couldn't find any words. It was too hot and he was staring at me and I didn't believe there would be no consequences. Left eye. I asked Letch, What did you say to your dad. I told him I thought he was a bastard, Letch said. I think you're a bastard, I said. Good, he said. Angel-Hair brought his hands out from behind his head and folded them in his lap. He asked, What did Letch do. Letch asked, What else. I just sat there. Letch said, Anything you'd like to get off your chest. Letch said, Now's the time, Rhonda. He said, Put your balls into it. I couldn't say anything. I didn't want to say anything too awful because I'd be seeing him later that night. And the next. And the next. Then Letch checked his watch and said, Time's up. He said, You sure fucked that up. He said, There's always next year. Right eye. We walked back to the car and went to Burger King. Consolation prize, he said. The other kids were always talking about Angel-Hair's horrendous limp, but I loved his wrists. If he even tried to clip his fingernails, the vibrations would buckle the bones in his hands. I imagined him with a fingernail file, working carefully, slowly, trying not to hurt himself. Just trying to file them all down without an amputation. And then an entire year went by and Letch took me back to the amnesty bench. Not to the day, but the same month. August. August meant that the Arizona summer was in its agonizing climax. The grocery store had fixed the awning. New. Shiny. Stripes, red and yellow.

The bench didn't hurt the backs of my thighs as I sat down. You remember how this works, Letch said. I think you're a bastard, I said. He slapped my cheek. Not too hard. One of his warning shots. Just a little pop to let me know I was close to pissing him off. We haven't started yet, he said. He checked his watch. Go, he said. Did the bench make you feel better, Angel-Hair asked. No, I said, but at least we were in public. He couldn't really hurt me in public. Left eye. I could imagine Angel-Hair flipping a coin and as it landed in his palm, his hand would fall off from his thin wrist, crumbling. I think you're a bastard, I said. You already said that, he said. Forty-five seconds left, he said. There were lots of people going into the store. Lots of people pushing piled-high shopping carts back to their cars. I wish I never met you, I said. I wish my mom never met you, I said. He laughed. I waited for him to say something nasty but all he said was, Thirty seconds. If I had a thumb war with Angel-Hair, if I pinned his thumb, if I mashed his thumb down as hard as I could, he'd probably start crying. Tell me more, he said. What else, Letch said. I hate you, I said. Good, he said. I hate you and I hate it when you touch me, you shouldn't touch me, I said. What else, he said. Angel-Hair asked, Weren't you scared. He locked his hands behind his head again. The curlicue stains standing out from his armpits. Why, I said. Why would I be scared, I said. Fifteen seconds, Letch said. Why would you believe him, Angel-Hair asked. Why would you believe that he wouldn't hurt you for the things you said on the amnesty bench, he said. Who said I believed him, I said. Right eye. I hope you die, I said to Letch. Ten seconds, he said. It felt like the last ten seconds in the whole world. I hope you die I hope you die I hope you die I hope you die I hope you die I hope you die I hope you die I hope, I said. Time's up, he said. Do you feel better, he said. Left eye. Letch took me out for a cheeseburger on our way home. He said, Good job. He said, You can get one with bacon.

HOME

I sat in the Neon, staring at the enormous orange wall, which was right where my house was supposed to be.

Me, Rhonda, confused and pissed off.

"Problem solved," little-Rhonda said.

"What's that supposed to mean?"

"You don't have to burn it down."

"You ever seen *Poltergeist*?"

"Have you?" he said.

"Obviously, if I'm asking."

"If you've seen it, I've seen it, remember?"

"Do you have to antagonize me right now?" I said. "Can't you see I'm a little rattled?"

"You were saying," he said, faking an apologetic tone.

"*Poltergeist* is about a housing project that's been built on top of a graveyard. But the land developers only removed the headstones and left the bodies in the ground. The bodies got mad and haunted the houses."

"There aren't any bodies buried here."

"I know that. What I'm saying is that the ground might be contaminated. The ground might still be haunted."

"With what?"

"I don't know. All I know is that the sidewinder's bite told me the only way to end all this was to burn the place down."

"How are you going to burn down a concrete building?"

"I'll need an explosion." I got out of my car.

"Right now?" he yelled after me. "You're going to blow it up right now?"

―――――

First thing I noticed when I walked in the automatic doors was a young woman wearing an orange vest, her hands in front of her bellybutton, folded into a prayer position. She smiled at everyone who walked in, which right now was just me, so she and I had a moment where we stared at each other, and it was hard to read her face, but I think she looked concerned.

"Twenty percent off area rugs today, sir," she said. "Are you thinking about purchasing an area rug?"

"I might be," I said, trying to fold my hands, too, but because of my bent arm, they didn't fit together like they were supposed to. A flip of the switch and furtive electricity wormed its way through my good hand. I put my fists in my pockets, fingered the book of matches.

This orange-vested woman and I kept staring at each other. She looked at my crooked arm, my eyes, crooked arm again before she said, "Area rugs are an instantaneous way to transform a room, sir."

Saying, "Sir, it turns something old into something new."

And finally, "Sir, you won't even recognize the place!"

―――――

I couldn't believe that most of Home Depot used to be open desert, couldn't believe that I used to hop over the fence in our backyard and spend hours trudging through the sand, shooting doves with shotguns. Bruise on my shoulder. Mark of a man. Letch pushing on it and smiling, proud of me. I couldn't believe that the sand took over our house, as the rooms moved away from one another, as they couldn't stand to be this close to us, the rooms splintering and leaving me alone to fend for myself.

Now I'd give the house what it deserved.

I decided to track down someone who worked here and ask some questions. I meandered down an aisle; its sides were displays of different drapes and curtains. I was surrounded by all the different shades of purple. Walking toward gray. Off-white.

About thirty feet ahead of me, there was a store clerk talking curtains with another customer. I lagged there, waiting for him. I touched the different fabrics. I wondered what was behind all these curtains. Lifted one up, expecting to see something unexpected, expecting to see Letch, but there were just hundreds of drapes, rolled up, waiting to be taken to houses and hung up in windows, to keep all the lewd secrets trapped inside.

"Can I help you?" The guy had snuck up on me.

"How long has this place been open?"

"Don't know," he said. "I've been here two months. Are you looking for new drapes?"

"Has it been here longer than five years?"

"Still don't know," he said, checking up and down the aisle, if anyone else needed his services.

"I used to live here.'"

"In Home Depot?"

"Home Depot was built on top of my house. I'm trying to find out when my house was knocked down."

I wondered if I was in the exact place where my bedroom used to be. The bikini girls. All the love I yanked from myself. Or maybe I stood where the bathroom used to be. The smell of hydrogen peroxide. Mom rubbing soaked socks or cotton balls or coffee filters on my shiners and singing one of her John Lennon songs in the softest voice in the universe.

"Has anything out of the ordinary happened here?" I said to the salesman.

He smirked, leaned in close to me, close enough that I knew he had barbecue sauce at lunch. "Got a lady's number last week. Took her to dinner." He flicked his eyebrows. "Then took her home."

"What about the floor?"

"Sir?"

"Has the floor ever moved? Stretched? Have the aisles ever gotten longer?"

My good hand got attacked from the inside, felt smothered in gunshots, like there was a tiny me and a tiny Letch walking through the desert, walking with our shotguns and aiming at the doves but missing, bullets imbedding into my hands.

"I'll be right back," the orange-vested salesman said, scurrying away.

I was all alone, the book of matches still in my pocket.

If they were here, hiding somewhere, maybe I should smoke them out. I mean, there I was surrounded by rolls and rolls of drapes and curtains, which was basically a huge cache of kindling, and I had a book of matches and I could feel the snake's venom bloating my veins, percolating, searing, ordering me to complete my mission, to find my mom and Letch and finish this.

I ducked behind one of the hanging curtains and sat on a stack of extra drapes, all rolled into thin tubes and covered in plastic casings to protect them. I struck a match. The first one lit the edges of four different curtains, and the second lit six, tried to stretch the next match to light eight and ended up burning my finger, a black smudge across my fingerprint.

It all started to take.

To smoke.

The burning plastic produced an awful smell, like singed hair, like old lady Rhonda's couch. I shimmied across the stacks of curtains, lighting the next group, and that was when the sand cracked the floor, pushing up through the concrete's slits. Sidewinders wiggling through the cracks, purring, purring.

And then I saw Letch. Sitting about twenty feet away from me. Sitting next to little-Rhonda, but he wasn't wearing his miner's helmet. Sitting on some rolled-up curtains.

Letch had antifreeze all over the front of his white shirt.

Me, Rhonda, watching them.

Suddenly they weren't sitting on the rolled-up curtains anymore. Suddenly they were sitting on the amnesty bench. Rickety wooden thing with a plastic red and yellow awning. Letch said, "You've got sixty seconds," and the kid said, "I think you're a bastard."

I ran over to them and tried to grab Letch, to scream at him, but they couldn't hear me, and he couldn't feel my hands on him.

He said to the kid, "Forty-five seconds."

He said, "You never were very good at this," laughing at the kid, laughing at me.

I leaned over so our faces were only inches from each other. I said, "Why won't you leave us alone?" but he still couldn't hear me. I shut my eyes. My good hand fingered the matches in my pocket. I could hear people in the store saying things: "Where's that smoke coming from?" and "I think something might be burning!"

Finally, Letch looked at me, not the kid, looked right in my eyes and said, "Nice arm," and he ran his fingers up my arm's bend, and I wanted to do something to stop him, but I have to tell you that I liked the way his fingers felt on me.

The fire alarm went off.

"Where is she?" I said.

"Your guess is as good as mine."

I peeked my head out into the aisle, noticed the customers stampeding toward the exits. The orange-vested drones, scattering in every direction, tried to locate the smoke's source.

I grabbed the kid's hand, helped him off the amnesty bench, told him, "You better get lost." He took off running toward an exit, looking over his shoulder at me, all confused, a look that seemed to ask if it might be better if he stayed around to help, but I had to do this on my own.

There were voices, working their way toward us, orange-vested voices no doubt, beginning to pinpoint the epicenter of all that was going wrong.

I looked at Letch and said it one last time, "I think you're a bastard."

"You can do better than that by now. Put your balls into it."

He'd taught me how to put my balls into things, and there was one last sequence of events that needed them: like striking a match and holding it to the amnesty bench's plastic red and yellow awning until it started to drip down on him. I put my balls into realizing that the only thing I had to burn today was him. Letch's face contorted into anger and he said, "What are you doing?" and I said, "I can finally do it," and he said, "Do what?" but I didn't answer, letting the awning melt, turning to hot wax, torture raining down on Letch, dousing him in color. He yelled and bellowed and shook his head around, trying to keep the freefalling colors out of his mouth, but the wax got so hot that it boiled on his skin. Violent, hysterical bubbles. Letch screamed, tried to get off the bench, but the wax, like glue, had fastened him to it and he couldn't move. He flailed his arms. I could see less and less of Letch as the colors smeared all over him.

I said, "Of course you love your own son," and Letch said, "You're not my son," which was true, but it didn't matter anymore. It didn't matter whose son I really was, because family could mean so many different things. It could mean anything. Maybe my mom was my mom, but maybe old lady Rhonda was my mom, or maybe there were no moms and there were no dads and there were no children, only people. Maybe that's enough.

The burning wax slathered all over Letch's face, dissolving his lips and eyes and nose, melting them to nothing, coating him in a red and yellow mask. I said, "Tell me where she is," and I could hear him trying to say things, but they were only mumbles mashed into the mask. I looked at him one last time: a statue, frozen, castrated. He was fixed to the amnesty bench, and

I wondered, did that mean he'd tell the truth forever?

The last thing I did was fuzz his head, which didn't have hair anymore, but felt smooth like a rubber ball, very hot, swirled in color.

I slipped out into the aisle, acted like a panicked customer, too, except I wasn't running away, wasn't fiending for an exit, I was running up and down different aisles, looking for her. If he was here, she was here. I tried to blend in with the mania, the roiling fear of everyone else. I saw their faces and made mine look petrified, slaloming down random aisles, camouflaging myself as another person trying to make it out alive.

I turned down another one. There were four display-kitchens set up. Sinks, countertops, cupboards. Refrigerators. Microwaves. Pots and pans hanging off racks. Expensive light fixtures dangling over the stoves.

I ran by the first three of them, jumping over huge cracks in the floor and massive piles of sand, sidewinders winding all around me, purring. And as I sprinted past the last kitchen, I saw my mom standing there, and she said, "Are you hungry?" reaching into the freezer, pulling out some taquitos. She smiled. "I can thaw these if you're hungry."

I stopped, walked over to her. "Where have you been?"

"I don't know, baby."

"Tell me."

Sidewinders slithered all around us.

Another cluster of panicked customers ran by, as we stood in the kitchen.

"I don't know what to tell you," she said, shaking a few taquitos onto a plate, placing them in the microwave.

The fire alarm wailed.

A man's voice came over a loud speaker, "Please go directly to an exit and leave the store in a calm and orderly manner."

She started to slowly sink in the sand underneath her. But she didn't even notice. The world, her life, her everything was changing all around and she wasn't even noticing. There were a thousand things I wanted her to tell me, a thousand things I had to ask, a thousand explanations I needed to get so I could save my fraying sense.

"We don't have much time," I said. "Tell me."

She fiddled with the buttons on the microwave, inching lower. "How long do I cook these for again? I can't remember, baby."

"Mom, answer me."

"I think it's a minute and a half." She pushed more buttons on the microwave. Inching. Inching. "But I can't say for sure."

"Mom!"

Inching.

"You don't remember, baby?" She'd sunk far enough that the microwave was out of her reach. "I'm sorry," she said. Her body getting lower and lower. Buried fast. Up to her waist. I grabbed her hands and tried to keep her from leaving, but I couldn't do anything to stop her. "I can't reach. You'll have to finish yourself."

Me, Rhonda, I couldn't do anything to make her stay.

Up to her chest.

"You can finish them yourself; I know you can," she said.

The man's voice came over the loud speaker, "Please leave the store immediately. This is an emergency situation."

"Don't go," I said to her. "Please don't."

She sank farther into the sand.

Up to her neck now.

She looked up at me. Just a face. A sinking sad face. A sinking sad face I'd never see again. "I'm sorry I couldn't stay with you," she said.

"Why couldn't you?"

"I'm sorry."

"Why?"

"I'm so sorry."

I heard a voice behind me, an orange-vested employee saying,

"Hey, man, come on. We have to get you out of here."

"I'll be there in a minute."

"Now."

"Just a second."

He came over and grabbed me by the shoulders.

"Let go!" I said.

"You have to get out of here."

With only one good hand, there was nothing I could do, no way to fight him off. He dragged me away. I called to her, "Why didn't you try and find me after I got out?" but she didn't answer, her face vanishing in the sand, her hair lying on top of it like a dead animal.

Then the last strands of her, the idea of her, were swallowed up.

"What's wrong with you?" the orange-vested employee said. "You have to get out of here!" and he dragged me, away from her, away from Letch, dragged me through the exit and left me on the sidewalk with all the other scared people.

HOME-COOKED MEAL #3

We were all together. Me, my mom, and Letch. She'd thawed another dinner, this time chicken burritos. She put the burritos on plates. Nothing else was on the plates, just those dry white rectangles. Letch frowned at it, looked at me, pretended to throw up. I laughed. She asked what the hell was so funny, you guys, but she knew we were joking about her crappy cooking and sometimes she'd joke about it, too.

Pretty soon we were all pointing at our burritos and laughing.

Letch said, "Doesn't this look scrumptious, Rhonda?"

I said, "Fit for a king."

She said, "This recipe has been passed down in my family for centuries."

I took a bite. Letch took a bite. She took a bite.

Letch, still chewing, said, "It's even more delicious than it appears."

I said, "This is the best thing I've ever tasted."

She said, "The trick is to microwave them for sixty seconds. A lot of people don't know that."

We were all laughing, but kept shoveling more burrito into our mouths.

Letch said, "Do you have some moral objection to salsa?"

I said, "It is a little dry."

My mom said, "Salsa?" and shrugged her shoulders. "I say the drier, the better."

We were still laughing.

"I hear what you're saying," Letch said to her, "but if I really, really wanted salsa, do you think it would ruin the dish?"

I said, "If the drier, the better, should I go outside and get some sand to throw on top?"

Letch leaned over and fuzzed my head.

My mom said, "Yes, please, sand sounds lovely."

Letch said, "I could go for some sand myself."

I said, faking a British accent, "I shall return," and went out back and hopped the fence: nothing but desert for as far as I could see. It was a warm night, not too hot. There was a quail sitting in a hole near the top of a cactus. I filled my pockets with sand and jumped the fence again. I walked back to the table.

Letch said, "Waiter, may I have some sand added to my entree?"

My mom said, "Me, too, please. I'm dying for some sand."

Still using the British accent, I said, "Ladies first," and walked over to my mom and asked, "Would you like the sand on the side or on top of your burrito?"

"I'd like it right on top."

I dumped a handful on her food.

We were really cracking up. My mom laughed so hard she was crying.

"Waiter, I'm waiting," Letch said.

"Sorry, sir," and strutted over to Letch. "Fancy some sand?"

"Does the queen fancy cock?" he said, right when my mom drank more tcha-bliss, and she laughed so hard that she spit and choked.

I shook sand all over his burrito and he said, "Thank you, kind sir," and I said, "No, thank you," and my mom said, "No, we insist! Thank you," and I bowed and said, "The pleasure was mine," and strutted back to my burrito and spread the rest of the sand all over it.

We picked up our sandy burritos and pretended to eat them.

"Just when I didn't think it could get any better!" I said.

"You were right, Rhonda," Letch said. "The sand really did the trick."

My mom said, "Sand is this year's pepper."

We howled, holding our sandy burritos.

Letch smacked the table and snorted, setting his burrito down. He said, "Anyone feel like making nachos?" and my mom and I told him, yes, we'd love some nachos and we all went into the kitchen. Letch spread chips on an oven pan. I grated cheese. My mom pulled out the salsa, shook it into a bowl, and Letch said, "Oh, sure, now there's salsa," and we kept on laughing.

HER SALIVA TASTED LIKE BLOOD

Me, Rhonda, with little-Rhonda, speeding up I-5 past all those dead seals. Doing ninety. Had been roaring up the freeway since leaving Phoenix, waiting to be pulled over, but it hadn't happened yet. And it didn't happen. We made it all the way to San Francisco without a squawk from the proper authorities.

We returned the rental car and walked back to my apartment. First thing I noticed when I walked in was a present, gift-wrapped in a newspaper page of stock quotes. Sitting on the burned couch. Written on its top, in a black marker, was this:

From: Rhonda
To: Rhonda

There was a small card propped against the package.

I looked at little-Rhonda and said, "You shouldn't have," and he said, "I didn't," so I opened the card:

We're celebrating.
You helped me out of the kindness of your heart.
Now it's my turn to give back.
I'll see you soon, Crash Man, R.

I hadn't expected anything from old lady Rhonda.

I looked at the little guy and said, "Thanks for nothing."

He flipped me the bird. "Are you two going to have a Rhonda-*vous*?"

I tore into the gift, throwing the paper on the floor and

opening the box. Inside, there was a receipt for an airline ticket to Burbank. For a month from now. I didn't understand why anyone would want to fly to Burbank, but I figured she'd fill in the gaps later and I didn't brush my teeth or take off my shoes, just crawled in bed and passed out with the lights on, like my mom used to do. Instead of my normal nightmare, I had a dream about an old Thanksgiving dinner, from when I was a kid: the time my mom thawed frozen lasagna, saying, "Not many people know this, but some of the Pilgrims were Italian." She didn't eat any herself, but disappeared with a glass of tcha-bliss, leaving me at the kitchen table alone. I tried to cut a bite, but it was still icy in the middle.

———

By the next morning, my normal nightmare was back. I'll tell you about it later. Someone pounded on my door, and I got out of bed, embarrassed that I still wore the clothes decorated in dumpster-clumps. "Who's there?"

"It's me, Crash Man," old lady Rhonda said. "Open up," which I did and she stood there holding a ratty suitcase, tucking her long gray hair behind her ears. Her split lip looked much better.

I panicked that she was disappearing, too, my good hand igniting in a violent radio static, the bent, dead one waiting for a miracle. "Where are you going?"

She rubbed my cheek, flattened a few curls on my head. "I'm staying here, baby. With you." She walked over to the burned couch, set the suitcase down, told me to sit and close my eyes. I did. I heard her unzip the suitcase and she yelled, "Open up!"

The suitcase was filled with money. Small bills. Twenties, tens, fives, ones.

"Did you go on 'Wheel of Fortune'?" I said.

"Not yet. But that's why we're going to Burbank. I'm on the show in five weeks."

"Congratulations. Where's the money from?"

"My husband ran off. He left me $6,000."

I was shocked: shocked that he had that kind of money and lived in this dump; shocked that he'd give any to Rhonda as he ran out of town. "Where did he go?"

"Not my problem anymore."

"Are you sad?"

"Do you want to know what we were fighting about when he hit me the other night?"

I didn't know if I really wanted to know, didn't want to hear about him being mean to her. But I loved hearing new things about old lady Rhonda so I said, "I guess."

"No. Forget it. I'm not ready to tell you."

"Why not?"

She changed the subject: "What happened on your big date?"

"Let's forget about that, too."

She laughed and said, "Fair is fair," and asked if I wanted to have dinner that night. "I've got something important to tell you."

"Great."

"You should change your outfit and take a shower before dinner," she said, laughing and holding her nose.

———

Being back home was really confusing, and I wish I could tell you that I did something that afternoon, that I went outside, that I looked for a job, but the truth is, I drank bourbon in bed. I stripped the sheets because I wanted to see Madeline's stain on the mattress and I rolled around, so confused about what was supposed to happen, what I was supposed to do. I'd seen my mom and watched her vanish for the last time and I'd seen Letch and burned him to the amnesty bench and I'd finally left that place for good. I was still thinking about Vern breaking my arm and Handa never wanting to see me again, and the whole world felt assaulting. I hated that people went to their jobs and shopped online. I hated that there were time zones and television stations. I hated professional sports and organic vegetables and fossil fuels. Everyone else knew how to put the bourbon down and get up off the mattress, but there was no way I could do it. I fell asleep like that. Woke up and it was dark outside.

———

Old lady Rhonda came in my apartment and started cooking. Two bottles of red wine sat on the small counter, uncorked. She poked her head out of the kitchen and asked if a certain sleepyhead was ready for a glass of *vino*.

When was the last time I'd had a glass of water?

"This is a celebratory dinner," she said, handing me my wine.

"What are we celebrating?"

"Two things"

"What?"

"Me and you."

We let our wine glasses collide; we swigged; we smiled.

"What's for dinner?" I said.

"I'm broiling steaks."

"Sounds perfect."

She rubbed the side of my face. "Good boy."

I sat down on the burned couch. I thought about the sidewinder that had bitten me and stood back up.

Old lady Rhonda saw me staring at the couch and asked, "Finally tired of it?"

"I guess," I said. "Can I help you cook?" I took a few steps toward the kitchen. I thought about Madeline, her Meat Trees, thought about Skyler, and wondered if they were somewhere right that very second doing the same thing as old lady Rhonda and me.

"Just sit down, baby. You can cook for me next time. Right now, I'm taking care of you."

"I make a mean dish called Meat Trees."

She smiled. "I can't wait to try them."

I sat back down, and minutes later, she put a plate in my lap. There wasn't anything else on the plate except the steak, cooked rare, shaped like a big bleeding tongue.

"Look at this," she said and handed me a shiny steak knife. "Picked a set of these up today." She tucked it between the plate and my thigh. She set the fork next to the steak.

"Did we miss 'Wheel of Fortune'?" I asked.

"You were asleep. I got every puzzle."

I stared at her, in a weird awe. On one hand, it was only "Wheel of Fortune," so who cares, but it was wonderful to watch someone shine at something.

I held the fork with my good hand, the knife with the warped one.

"I forgot the wine bottles," she said, going back to the kitchen and getting them. Old lady Rhonda sat down next to me. She sliced a bite of steak and put it in her mouth. She scrunched her face in delight. "I know my way around a steak."

I switched hands, deciding that the knife should be in my good one, so I could generate enough force to saw through the bloody meat.

Then I switched back.

Did it again.

She took another bite and said, "What are you waiting for?"

"Nothing," I said, holding the fork in my dead hand. I stabbed the steak with the fork to hold it still. With my other hand, I used the knife to saw at the meat, trying to get through it, but my other arm was too weak, couldn't hold the steak steady in one place. It slid all over the plate. I switched hands again, but my bent arm didn't have the strength to cut through the meat, just scratched shallow trenches in its browned top.

"Oohh," old lady Rhonda said, "this will be fun."

"What?"

"Let me help you."

"I can do it," I said, because I'd been feeding myself since I'd broken my arm. I just hadn't eaten anything that took two hands, usually soup or chili or SpaghettiOs: an entire diet from the dusty shelves of liquor stores. I'd braced the cans between my legs as I spun the opener around the rims.

"You have to let me," she said. "As a favor."

I mauled the meat one last time, hoping I could do it myself, but it was no use. Part of me wanted to throw the fork and knife across the room, but I handed them to old lady Rhonda, who smiled. She cut a little piece of meat and buzzed it in front of my face, flying it in zigzag patterns and making zooming airplane noises. "Open the hangar!" she said.

I ate it up.

"I really wanted kids," she said. "I had seven sisters. There was always something fun going on in that house. Not like me and his place upstairs. So morose. We were barely married. Just walked by each other on our way to the bathroom."

Another bite wiggled through the sky, doing tricks, old lady Rhonda making swooping sounds. This chunk of meat was a little sinewy so I swallowed it without really chewing.

"How long were you two like that?"

"Long time. We hadn't had sex in almost twenty years. When we first got married, I felt irreplaceable. And slowly I went from being important to the most irritating woman in the world."

She cut herself a bite and stuck it in her mouth. I took a huge sip of wine.

"You're not irritating," I said.

This time she didn't make any airplane sounds, sticking the fork up to my face until I stripped it clean.

"Thanks," she said. "Are you going to tell me about your date?"

"I don't think I can."

"That bad?"

There weren't words for what I'd felt that night with Handa. If there were words, I didn't know them. I'd never heard them. No one had ever taught me the words to detail a situation like that. All I could say to old lady Rhonda was, "Humiliating," but I knew that was only a shard of what I felt. Then: "She said she never wants to see me again."

"I'm sorry, baby," old lady Rhonda said, rubbing my leg. "Why is that?"

I wanted to tell her. I really did. But I wasn't willing to chance that once she heard about the dumpster, the trapdoor, the wine puddles, that she'd leave me, too. "I don't want to talk about it."

"You can tell me anything."

"Can we talk about something else?"

"Do you want another bite of steak?"

I nodded. She cut me one and flew it toward my mouth. "Please, don't ever tell me something that you don't want to," she said, "but I hope you know, I'll never judge you."

Me, Rhonda, I wanted to believe her, wanted to purge and tell her every contaminated thing I'd done. The top secret. The buried and ugly and hideous. But also the harmless, the bland. I wanted to believe that no matter the caste of syllables that came from my mouth, she'd understand me.

I talked with a mouthful of meat: "I believe you."

"You want to believe me, Crash Man. But I don't think you do yet."

I swallowed.

She cut me one more bite and flew it around in front of my face. "Mayday," she said, lowering the bite so it almost smashed into my lap. "Mayday. We're losing altitude!" She pulled it up and I took it in. "I'll prove to you that you can say anything to me, okay?"

"Okay."

"Remember when I didn't want to tell you what my husband and I were fighting about? We were fighting about you."

"Why?"

"Because you're the son I never had," she said. She leaned over and hugged me, kept me pressed against her. I could feel her heartbeat knocking against me. I'll never make you understand, but being in her arms felt like I was in the womb, surrounded by its wet protection.

"That night with Handa," I said, "I scared her."

"How?"

I didn't answer.

"No matter what it is, please tell me," she said.

"I don't think I can."

"You can."

"Are you sure?"

"I'm sure."

And I told her everything about that night. And she kept me in her arms the whole time.

STOP MAKING MY LIFE SO HARD

I'd like to tell you one of my favorite memories of my mom. The day she told me I'd overslept and that I was about to miss the school bus, that I needed to get to the bus stop ASAP because she didn't have time to drive me to school.

I said, "Why?" and she said, "If I'm late again, I'm getting fired."

I didn't want to have anything to do with her losing another job, so I skipped the shower, but brushed my teeth and combed my hair a little. I got dressed as fast as I could and didn't eat anything for breakfast even though I was hungry, but it was serious business if she got fired, and I said to her, "Bye, Mom," and walked to the bus stop with three minutes to spare.

My stomach growled, but maybe I could bum a bite from another kid on the bus.

But three minutes went by and the bus wasn't there, which wasn't unheard of, this was the school bus and sometimes the school bus was late. I hoped I hadn't read the clock wrong on my way out the door. It was obvious that three minutes had gone by. It felt more like six or seven minutes. Still no bus. My stomach growled. I walked to the corner to peek for the bus.

Our garage door went up and my mom backed her car out. As she was driving up our street, she pulled over next to me and said, "Did you miss the bus?"

"I was three minutes early," I said, and she said, "Then where is it?" and I said, "Maybe it's still coming," and she said, "Jesus

Christ," and I said, "I swear I was here early," and she said, "Just get in."

We drove. She sped, weaving in between cars, honking. She smoked and flicked the butts out the window.

"If I lose my job," she said, but never finished her thought, just kept saying that, over and over, "If I lose my job…" and "If I lose my job…"

I was starving and kept saying, "Sorry, Mom."

"I don't want you to be sorry," she said. "I want you to stop making my life so hard."

There was a clock on her radio, and I watched it, trying to slow the numbers down with my mind. I looked at green stoplights as we drove up to intersections and tried to keep the lights green, too. I tried to do everything I could think of to help, because I didn't want her to lose another job, and I didn't want it to be my fault.

We approached the last stop light before my school. It was green. I focused on it. I told it, please, you have to help me, you don't know what will happen if she doesn't make it.

I tried to reason with this light, to level with it, to show it our side of things.

But it wasn't listening. It went yellow. Red. My mom went, "Shit."

I counted every second until it went green again. Mom lit another cigarette. The veins in her arthritic hands looked like blue pens.

We turned right onto my school's street. I already had my backpack in hand. I said, "Just pull over and I'll jump out," and she said, "Okay," and I said, "I'm so sorry for this morning," and she said, "Don't worry," and I said, "No really, Mom, I'm so sorry if I ruined your job," and she said, "Just forget it," and we pulled up in front of my school, and the entire parking lot was empty.

There weren't any buses. Any cars.

There weren't any students or teachers walking around.

The place was completely deserted.

I looked at her, and she had this huge smile on her face.

She said, "I got you!" and I said, "What?" and she said, "It's Saturday, silly."

I didn't understand what was happening.

She told me that she'd made the whole thing up as a joke: she'd decided to wake me up instead of letting me sleep in so she could play a little trick on me. She said, "Were you surprised?" and I said, "Yeah," and she said, "You didn't have any idea?" and I said, "No way," and she said, "I got you good," and she leaned over and tickled me, and I never minded being tickled, even though sometimes her nails were rough on my skin.

"How about breakfast?" she said, and I said, "You don't have to work?" and she said, "We've both got the day off."

We went to a diner, and I ate a sausage omelet while mom drank black coffee and kept on smoking. Every once in a while she'd excuse herself to go to the bathroom, but I didn't mind. The bathroom was in the back, and there wasn't a door near there. I knew she couldn't disappear until we left. I ate my omelet as slow as I could.

THAT ANIMAL

The next morning, I had a hankering for Lucky Charms. Old lady Rhonda asked me for my wallet, said she left her money upstairs but not to worry, she'd pay me back.

"You don't have to do that," I said.

"Once you're cooking again, you can buy the cereal. Until then, I'm your sugar-mama buying sugary cereal." She also said she felt like mimosas, and she'd be back in ten minutes for Lucky Charms and cocktails.

I stayed on the burned couch, dozing.

———

I had my nightmare. I'm still working up the courage to tell you about it.

When I finally heard the front door open and close, it wasn't her, but little-Rhonda. "Good morning, sunshine," he said.

"Old lady Rhonda is coming right back," I said. "Don't you have something else to do?"

"Are you getting rid of me?"

"I'm trying."

———

My neck hurt from the charred couch so I crawled over to my mattress, which was still streaked in Madeline's entrails. I let my hand linger over her blot, but I have to tell you that I didn't feel sad. I didn't see the stain and feel defeated. And once I'd seen the stain, my good hand didn't shimmy like a possessed maraca. Yes, I thought of Madeline, I missed Madeline, but I was all right. There was no Letch haunting me. No Lyle ignoring or hurting old lady Rhonda. Just me and her, two people who'd been segregated from happiness.

———

An hour later she still wasn't back and I worried something had happened. I put some clothes on and walked downstairs to our usual liquor store.

"You seen Rhonda?" I asked the guy.

"Half an hour ago."

"Did she say where she was going?"

"No, but they seemed like they were fighting."

"They?"

"Her and Lyle."

"Lyle's gone."

"He was just here."

"Are you sure?"

"I've known Lyle a long time."

"And he was just here?"

"Rhonda started buying this," the guy said, tapping a box of Lucky Charms, some OJ, and champagne. They sat behind the counter. "But then Lyle walked in and said he had to talk to her right now."

"Was he mad?"

"How do I know?"

"Was he yelling?"

"No."

"Was he aggressive?"

"Like what?"

"Did he grab her?"

"Yes."

"Where?"

"The elbow."

"Was she hurt?"

"How do I know?"

"Did she look hurt?"

"She looked fine."

"What do you mean 'fine'?"

The guy picked up a remote control and flipped on a little TV. "She didn't look hurt."

"Are you sure?"

"No."

"No?"

He changed channels, zooming through them, stopping on a soccer game. "I don't know. She looked normal, okay?"

"Then what?"

"Then they left."

"Did they say where they were going?"

"No."

"Did they go to their apartment?"

"I don't know!" he said and fiddled with the TV's volume until it was so loud people could probably hear soccer blaring in the lower Haight.

———

I was back in my apartment. Pacing. Opening and closing my good fist as it shuddered with angry life. There was a knife lying on the counter. It wasn't that sharp, but if I had to, I could take it upstairs to defend myself. "Where are you?" I said, hoping little-Rhonda would answer me, that he'd help me figure out what was supposed to happen next. Should I go up there and pound on the door? Should I hold the knife behind my back?

It was the only knife I owned. I used it for everything. I sliced cheese for *quesadillas*. I used its tip as a screwdriver, its handle as a hammer.

Then my toilet flushed, and little-Rhonda walked out carrying the newspaper. He looked at me, knew something was wrong, and said, "What?"

"Her husband's back."

"And?"

"He took her," I said, and as soon as the words wormed their way out of my mouth, my hand took off buzzing at mach speeds because I was convinced I'd never see her again. That he'd hurt her. Or hold her hostage. That he'd say, "We're still married and I want to work things out," and she'd say, "I love Rhonda like a son," and he'd say, "Not if I have anything to do with it," and if I never saw old lady Rhonda again it would be the worst disappearing act of them all.

"Took her where?" little-Rhonda said.

"Upstairs, I think."

"What are you going to do?"

"Should I kill him?"

"How do you know he took her?"

"The guy at the liquor store heard Lyle tell her he needed to talk."

"So they're just talking."

"Why would he come back just to talk?"

"I don't know."

"Help me figure out what to do."

He flipped his light, off, on, off, then left it on. "Go up there."

"I'll go up there."

"Go up there, knock, and see what they're doing."

"I'll knock and see what they're doing."

I walked toward the door and picked up the knife.

"Leave that," little-Rhonda said.

"I'll leave it for now."

My feet moved and my legs moved, carrying my crooked arm, my buzzing hand, my legs carrying every part of me, and I could kill her husband because no one was going to hurt her. My feet and legs carried me to the stairs and I sprinted up the stairs and I sprinted down the hall, sprinted right up to their door, pounding on it.

No answer.

I pounded.

Nothing.

Pounding.

Then footsteps.

Then old lady Rhonda's voice talking through the door, "Who is it?"

"Are you okay?"

"I can't talk right now."

"What's going on?"

"I can't talk."

"Are you all right?"

And I heard Lyle yell, "She can't talk!"

And the footsteps retreated from the door.

There were whispers between them.

I pounded again.

No answer.

Pounding.

Nothing.

Pounding.

Nothing.

I said, "I'm not leaving until you tell me what's going on."

Footsteps.

Old lady Rhonda said, "I'm fine. I'll talk to you later," and I said, "Will you open the door?" and she said, "I'll talk to you later," and I said, "I need to talk to you now."

Footsteps, heavier, jabbing their way toward the door, and Lyle saying, "Get out of my way."

"Leave him alone," she said.

"Then tell him to get out of here."

A feeling in my good hand like its walls were being pulverized by a sledgehammer.

"I'll talk to you later," old lady Rhonda said to me.

"I want to know you're okay," I said.

Someone punched the other side of the door. "Leave us alone!" Lyle said.

I punched the door back, creating gunshots in my good hand.

Old lady Rhonda told him she'll handle this and to please go back in the other room, and the cruel noises of his feet as he stomped away.

"Rhonda, don't," old lady Rhonda said. "Please go."

"I don't want to."

"But I need you to."

"You have my wallet."

"I'll give it to you later."

"But – "

"Go!" she said, and her footsteps retreated back into their apartment.

I stood there, my good hand in a fist to pound on the door again, but I didn't know what to do. Was I crying? I needed the knife, and old lady Rhonda said she didn't need my help, but I didn't believe her. She did need it. She was just scared. Maybe he'd hit her. Or threatened to. She only told me to leave to protect herself from another of his attacks, but she couldn't protect herself, I needed to protect her. Me, Rhonda, I needed to make sure nothing else happened to her.

I bolted back downstairs to my apartment and threw the door open and little-Rhonda said, "What happened?" and I said, "He's got her trapped in there," and he said, "Did you talk to her?" and I said, "He's got her so scared," and he said, "How did it end up?" and I said, "It hasn't ended yet."

I picked up the knife and turned toward the door, but little-Rhonda said, "Talk to me," and I said, "She needs me," and he said, "Sit down for a sec," and I went over to the burned couch and sat down next to him, holding the knife in my hand.

"So you're going up there to kick the door down and stab Lyle?"

"Yes."

"That's your plan?"

"That's my plan."

"You'll go to jail."

"She needs me."

"She doesn't need you in jail."

"She needs someone to rip that animal out of her life."

He turned his helmet's light off. "But we love her. Don't do something so we'll never see her again."

"What am I supposed to do?"

"Help her, but not this way."

"How can I help her?"

"We'll think of something," little-Rhonda said, but he didn't know, and I didn't know, and we went quiet, sitting on the couch. I still had the knife in my hand.

TELL ME MORE

Right eye. Can we talk about your mom, he said. Sure, I said. Did she call, I said. Does she want to visit me, I said. Left eye. She didn't call, he said. I knew she hadn't called. She'd never called. Never written. Never trained a carrier pigeon to fly to Angel-Hair's window and drop a message on the floor that I'd pick up on my way back to my room, a message I'd read over and over, never stopping, just reading. What if she had called, he said, and asked to speak with you. What would you want to say to her, he said. I'd ask where she's been. Where do you think she's been. I think she's mad at me. Right eye. She'd never written, never called, never stood outside the hospital's walls with a megaphone, screaming at me, asking me how I was doing. Never learned sign language and flashed me messages through the windows. Why is she mad at you, Angel-Hair said. Because of what I did, I said. She'd never played the game Telephone with a bunch of the kids from the hospital. Remember the game Telephone? I said. You whispered a secret to someone and then they told it to someone else who told it to someone else who told it to someone else, and by the time the last person got the message the words were wrong. My mom could have told a kid who lived at the end of the hospital's hall, who could have passed it on, the message snaking from kid to kid until finally someone came up to me and told me they had a message from my mom and the kid would whisper in my ear, I've always loved you. What did you do to make her mad, Angel-Hair said. I remember my first Christmas and my first birthday in here with Angel-Hair. I remember wondering if my mom still lived in the drifting house, or if she fled. I remember thinking that maybe she was somewhere missing me because now I was somewhere she couldn't see me if she decided she wanted to. Left eye. I hurt Letch, I said. How'd you hurt Letch, he said. Never wrote, never called, never thrown her voice like a ventriloquist into one of the orderlies or nurses or teachers walking up to me and saying, Baby, it's me. I'd ask, Mom. She'd say through some other person's mouth, Yes, baby, it's me, I've missed you. I'd ask, You have, you really have. And she'd say, Of course I have. Right eye. Angel-Hair said, What did you do to Letch. I said, He hurt me. Angel-Hair said, What did you do to Letch. Maybe my mom could hire a pilot to write her message in the desert sky so I'd be able to see it no matter where I was, words sprawling in the air. Angel-Hair said, You're not answering my question. My hands felt heavy with rocks, like they were going to stretch my arms and drag on the floor. When he'd ask me about Letch I'd get these fireflies jittering in my periphery and a feeling like I might faint. Right eye. Did you hurt Letch, Angel-Hair said. My mom used to write me messages all the time. She'd write them on the backs of old pizza boxes in a black magic marker. They'd say, Back on Friday. They'd say, See you on Tuesday. They'd say, Have a great weekend, and next to her messages there'd be money thumbtacked to the old pizza boxes, money so I could order new pizza boxes. Whenever Angel-Hair asked me about what happened to Letch, my hands turned into tiny cement mixers, weight spinning and flopping and shifting around inside of them. And there would be fireflies dancing next to my eye sockets. And I'd feel like at any second someone might bury me in sand. Left eye. One of her notes on a pizza box said, Gone fishin', and when she got home, I thought it would be funny to ask her if she caught any fish, but all she said was, What the hell are you talking about. Angel-Hair said, Please tell me what happened to Letch. I never knew how fast cement mixers could spin until my hands turned into them, until I felt my hands spinning faster than tires on the highway, the cement tumbling so fast. And there were the fireflies flying next to my eye sockets. And I felt like someone might bury me in sand. My hands went wild with wet cement. I looked at them and I looked at Angel-Hair and he said, Are you having those feelings in your hands. I said, Make them stop. He wrote something down. He said, Can you tell me what you were thinking or feeling right before they started. I watched my hands. I said, What were you saying about my mom. I said, Is she coming. I said, Did she write. I said, Does she still blame it all on me. Can you answer my question about your hands, he said. But there was no way I could because the cement mixers started going faster than space shuttles and all the fireflies flew right in my eye sockets and I couldn't see anything and couldn't feel anything except my hands and I fell out of my chair and Angel-Hair ran over.

ALONE AGAIN

Little-Rhonda and I sat around the apartment, but it wasn't long before I got antsy and said, "I'm going back up there," and he said, "I don't think that's a good idea," and I said, "I don't care what you think," and he said, "Will you leave the knife here?" and I said, "Why would I leave the knife here?" and he said, "So you don't do anything stupid," but I grabbed the knife and walked toward the door, little-Rhonda yelling after me, "Please don't do this."

Some tiny sidewinders slithered through my good hand. I put the knife in my dead one and held it behind my back. I didn't knock as hard this time. They didn't answer. I knocked a little harder, but they still didn't come to the door. I put a little more verve in my knock, but I want you to know that I was calm, only knocking harder in case they hadn't heard me. No one answered.

"Rhonda, it's me," I said.

Still nothing.

I didn't know whether to knock or yell or go away. I didn't even know if they were still in there. Then quiet footsteps coming to the door. The deadbolt flipped. The knob turned. The door creaked open a few inches. The security chain still latched. Old lady Rhonda peeked out.

"I need you to go downstairs," she said.

I had the knife behind my back. "Is he hurting you?"

"I'm fine."

"Can I come in?"

"No."

"Why did he come back?"

"Will you go downstairs?"

"Why's he here?"

"We can talk later."

"Are you two getting back together?"

She looked at me, pursed her lips. "I can't talk right now." Whispering: "I don't know what's going to happen, but I need you to leave."

"Why?"

"He and I need some time to talk."

"Why?"

"We've been together a long time."

"But you weren't happy."

Old lady Rhonda, still whispering: "Will you please leave?"

"I thought I made you happy."

"You do."

"And you love me."

"Yes."

"And I love you."

"I can't talk right now," she said.

"Can I have my wallet back?"

"I'll give it to you later. Here." She reached into her pocket and handed me a twenty. "This will tide you over," and she shut the door, her footsteps stepping away and I was alone again.

————

Me, Rhonda, getting another dose of the disappearing act. Me, still standing at old lady Rhonda's door, though she'd shut and locked it two hours ago. I stood there for two hours and no one cared. Old lady Rhonda didn't care. Karla didn't care. Handa didn't care. My mom didn't care. Two hours ago old lady Rhonda had shut it and walked back to him, and for two hours

I stood with the knife behind my back, praying she'd unlock the door and take me in her arms. I needed to be somewhere safe, contained, nurturing. Standing there, hoping to hear them talk, hoping for clues, a way to understand why she was doing this. Me, Rhonda, ripped up inside like Valencia Street, construction crews chiseling and pounding. And I was tired of being obliterated.

Me, kicking around a terrible notion. Knowing what I needed to do. I turned and walked down the stairs and came out on the street. It was dark outside. I tossed the knife to the ground. I ran down Valencia, toward Damascus, toward Vern. I was ready to beg for his forgiveness. Ask for one more chance. Pleading, "Please, I'll do anything if you'll break my arm."

———

I took a tiny detour, walking toward Handa's store. I stepped on another stenciling: *Satan has soft lips.* It was night so I knew Handa wouldn't be there. I wanted to see the place that used to make me feel better. I walked by and no one was inside, except her father, on his knees near the front door, stocking cans of chili. I wanted to go in there, buy some Magnums, and have everything be okay, but it wouldn't work, not anymore. I wanted her to forgive me and let me run my hand over the haze of hairs that wrapped around her belly button. Vern, only Vern was going to make me feel better. I knew he'd be mad and disgusted when I first walked into Damascus, but I knew he'd see it as a win/win once he got to smash my bone.

I stood outside the liquor store for a few minutes, thinking about Handa, another thing I'd ruined. And now it was time for Vern to help me.

"Hey, Rhonda!" little-Rhonda yelled. He stood across the street, flashing his helmet's light off and on. "Do you know Morse code?" The palm trees that decorated the middle of Dolores Street hissed, purred a noise as the wind hurtled through the fronds. His hat still flashed. He said, "This is an S-O-S."

There was a break in the traffic and I crossed the street, saying, "What's an S-O-S?" and he said, "You are."

"I'm going to Damascus."

"I won't let you."

"What?"

"I won't let you do this."

"You can't stop me."

"I'm the only person who can stop you," he said. He wasn't fiddling with his light anymore. Leaving it blazing. He must have put a new bulb in there, with higher wattage, because it blinded me.

"Well, I'm going," I said, and he said, "No, you're not."

I tried to walk by him.

"Don't make me do this," he said.

"There's nothing you can do," but little-Rhonda reached into his pocket and pulled out a sidewinder.

"What are you doing?"

"Saving me from you." He swung the sidewinder at me like a whip. The snake dug its fangs into my bent arm. I screamed, tried to run away, but I couldn't get out of the snake's bite.

A girl across the street looked at me, and I said, "Help!" but she didn't help me, walking faster to get away.

"I can't let you go to Damascus," little-Rhonda said. "I won't let Vern break that arm."

"Let go of me!"

But he didn't. Instead he used the snake as a leash, dragging me down the street.

"Where are you taking me?" I said.

"Home."

I couldn't believe that the last person in the solar system who hadn't betrayed me was doing this. "Why won't you help me?"

"I am."

"I want him to do it."

"We're going home."

"Let me go."

He kept tugging so I went limp, falling to the ground. I didn't think there was any way that little-Rhonda could drag all my weight, but he didn't slow down.

"Please," I said, "let him hurt me."

We passed a couple guys smoking out front of a bar. I held my bent arm up so they could see the snake's fangs, ripping my skin. I screamed at them, "Will you help me?"

"Help you what?" they said.

"Please help!"

But they turned their backs on me.

Little-Rhonda pulled me along.

"Let him hurt me," I said. "I want him to hurt me."

"I won't listen to another word," little-Rhonda said, reaching into his pocket and pulling out another sidewinder. This one launched at my face, its fangs puncturing my upper and lower lips, pinching them together like a muzzle. He towed me down Valencia, all the way to our dumpster.

TELL ME MORE

Over the days, months, years, Dr. Angel-Hair kept telling me that the house didn't move – that houses don't move, it's impossible – you imagined everything. Left eye. It isn't your fault, he said. The mind adapts to survive, he said. We were in his office. Again. Still. Words, so many words. It was raining out the window, on the other side of the metal grating, the window in the middle of all his diplomas. I was taking classes in the hospital. Working toward my GED. Yes, yes, he kept squashing these things, and the more he squashed them, the more I believed them. Believed him. I loved him. I loved that he wanted to help me, and I'd been in trouble when I first got there because I kept trying to masturbate during our sessions. I wanted to love myself in front of him. I wanted him to know that I could love myself. I could be a son. Could he be my father. My mom was gone and Letch was gone and there was no one left to love me. I liked the classes I took. Especially history. I liked reading the Greek myths. Right eye. I liked the idea of Sisyphus rolling his boulder up a hill forever. Rolling it right to the top and then having to start over at the bottom. I liked the way he got what was coming to him. The way they all did. And then some other time in his office, reeking of tuna fish. Again. Still. Without rain out the windows. Tell me, he said. Tell me about the night you poisoned Letch. We'd already talked about this many times. Tell me why you thought it was okay to hurt him, he said. I didn't think it was okay, I said. Then why did you do it, he said. Why did he do it, I said. Left eye. But he kept asking me, every day, every month. He kept asking me, why did you do it. I kept a journal. It was Angel-Hair's idea. It would help me get some of my secret feelings out. Writing could do that, he said. I wrote down all the stuff I didn't understand, the memories that seemed so real but I knew were impossible. Snakes didn't protect me. The house's rooms never lost their anchoring and drifted around the desert. And why did you think these things happened, he asked. I knew the answer. He'd told me the answer. Personalization, I said. No, he said. What, I said. *De*personalization, he said. *De*personalization, I said. Great, he said. Great work, he said. Right eye. We worked on how to say that word, what the word meant, what the word meant to me. Words sometimes mean different things to different people. All the days, months, years funneled themselves into one afternoon when I was eighteen and I was allowed to go outside, on the other side of the metal grating. I could leave. I'm fixed, I asked. You're going to be fine, he said. I scribbled in my journal a lot about my mom. I wrote poems about her, little stories, tried to remember happy times, wondered if she still went on disappearing acts. I didn't know if I missed her or if I missed the idea of another mom. The teacher always called on me during the classes. There were four other kids. We did algebra and I was the first to know the coefficient. The cosine. I was the first to solve equations with multiple variables. Right eye. I can leave, I asked him. Yes, he said. Stay in touch, he said. If you need anything, he said. We hugged. There was an English class. I loved reading *Brave New World*. In the book, people swallowed Soma. It was a pill. It was a pill to make them happy. I swallowed Klonopin. Is it like Soma, I asked Angel-Hair. Yes and no, he said. Left eye. I wrote a paper about swallowing Soma and my teacher told me it moved her. She was all bangs and a big nose and sturdy hips. Six feet tall. She had a thick German accent that made her sound mean. No matter what she was saying. And she was usually saying nice things. Complimenting us. Encouraging us. But the accent made me think of Nazis, death chambers disguised as showers. Dr. Angel-Hair said, Make me proud. He'd arranged for me to see a therapist in Phoenix who'd make sure I kept talking and swallowing pills. He'd arranged for me to rent a room from an old colleague of his, arranged for me to have a part-time job. At a drug store. Tell me, he said. Are you excited, he said. Make smart decisions, he said. Be patient, he said. You're going to be fine, he said. You're going to be great, he said. Don't do anything I wouldn't do. Don't fall in with the wrong crowd. Don't forget everything that's happened. Don't forget everything we've talked about. Love yourself.

SOME THINGS THAT BENT THE WORLD FOR ME

We were in front of the dumpster, little-Rhonda standing and me sprawled on the ground. The sidewinders were still latched to me: one holding my mouth shut, the other a leash sticking out of my bent arm. Little-Rhonda held each of the snakes' tails.

"I'll take the one off your lips," he said, "if you promise to keep calm."

I nodded.

The sidewinder released me, coiling itself and purring next to me.

My mouth didn't hurt. I rubbed my lips, expecting there to be blood or piercings, but there was nothing.

"One more thing you need to see down there," he said.

I didn't answer him, didn't know what to say after he'd dragged me here. I cleaned all the garbage out of the dumpster and opened the trapdoor. Started climbing the ladder, but I only made it five rungs down, and when I reached for the sixth, it felt thin, brittle, and it shattered and I fell. I fell, and I screamed, and then I landed in a huge pool of freezing tcha-bliss. I wasn't being pulled down through it this time, had to swim myself, swim down to the window at the bottom. I looked through it and saw little-Rhonda, again without his miner's helmet.

As soon as my feet hit the glass, they locked into something, and I couldn't move, my feet attached to some sort of conveyor belt, which pulled me above the kid. I followed everywhere he went, through the fractured house, desert everywhere. I followed above him as he went into the kitchen to make another Bloody Maria. He didn't fill the glass up all the way, leaving a few inches at the top of it. Me, Rhonda, following above him into the garage, as he grabbed the antifreeze. I followed him as he poured some of it into the Bloody Maria, stirring it all together, adding more pepper, more Tabasco. Following as he walked back toward the bedroom, trudging past cacti, Joshua trees, chollas, sidewinders. Toward Letch. Handing him the drink.

"Did you put your balls into it?" Letch said.

The kid didn't answer him, turned to leave Letch alone with his drink. The kid walking out, and I was getting pulled above him, out of the room, and I have to tell you that I didn't want to follow the kid, wanted to stay there and watch Letch drink the antifreeze, wanted to watch him take a big slurp.

The kid walked to his room. The kid crying. Breaking down. Hands over his face. Rubbing his eyes hard. Two purring sidewinders at his feet. I leaned down, my fingers scraping on the glass, knocking on the window, trying to get the kid's attention, but he couldn't hear me. Not yet. The kid getting down on the floor. The kid said to the snakes, "What did I do?"

He got up off the floor, walked back to Letch's bedroom, my body grazing on the glass above him. The kid said, "I don't think I made you a very good drink," and Letch said, "It's fine," and the kid said, "Give me that one, and I'll make you a new one," and Letch said, "Don't worry about it, Rhonda," and the kid said, "Please," and Letch said, "Get the hell out," and the kid said, "But I didn't put my balls into making that one," and Letch said, "It tastes fine so scram."

The kid walking back into the hallway. Crying again. The kid walking through the house's desert. Some ants ate a dead bird, carried specks of meat back to their home. The kid went all the way to the kitchen. The kid picked up the phone. The kid dialed 9-1-1. The kid said, "Someone's been poisoned," and the operator said, "Who?" and the kid said, "My mom's boyfriend. Send an ambulance," and the operator said, "Is he breathing?"

and the kid said, "I don't know," and the operator said, "Can you tell me what happened?" and the kid hung up.

He sat at the kitchen table. Wondering if Letch was still alive. I knocked on the glass again, but the kid didn't look up at me.

Minutes later, faster than the kid ever expected help to arrive, there was a siren screeching outside. Knocks on the door. The kid opened it. Two men standing there. One carrying a box. The kid said, "He's in the back," and pointed toward Letch's bedroom. The men hurrying down the hall. The kid following. They pushed the bedroom door open. Letch was sprawled out on the bed, holding his Bloody Maria, only a quarter of it left in the glass. He'd thrown up all over the front of his white t-shirt. He was sweating, shaking, head lolling.

The men ran over to him. One took the Bloody Maria from Letch's hand. The other said to the kid, "What did you use?"

"I didn't do anything."

Letch threw up again.

"You have to tell us what you used, so we can help him."

"I don't know," the kid said.

In the meekest voice I'd ever heard him use, Letch said: "I'm not... so good," and coughed, blood coming out of his mouth.

"Tell us!" the men said.

"Antifreeze."

"How much?"

The kid didn't answer.

"You're in a lot of trouble, son," one of the men said. "Help us."

Still not answering.

"How much?"

The kid held his thumb and forefinger a couple of inches apart.

"Jesus," the other man said, reaching inside the box and pulling out a long tube and a water bottle. Then he rolled Letch on his side, saying, "Sir, we're going to have to pump your stomach."

Letch didn't answer.

"Sir?"

The tube snaked down Letch's throat. One of the men held a water bottle up above Letch's head, forcing a liquid into Letch, who gagged and heaved and flailed his arms.

The kid crying.

The men worked on Letch, and the kid wandered back through the desert, down the hallway, finally sitting on the floor in his room. I was right above him, and I knew he couldn't hear me, but I didn't care, saying, "Things can get better."

The kid looked up. "Hello?"

"Can you hear me?" I said.

"Is someone there?"

"I'm right here."

"Hello?"

"I'm here."

"Hello?" he said, wiping the tears from his face, finally looking away from the ceiling.

When the police came and took the kid away, it was the only time I didn't follow him, couldn't follow him. My feet unfroze from the glass, and I floated back up to my life.

———

I climbed out of the dumpster.

"What did you see?" little-Rhonda said.

"I saw us try and poison him."

"Really?"

"Yeah."

"Do you wish he died?"

"I don't know."

"Tell me."

"I used to," I said, "but now I just wish we never met him."

We walked past a bulldozer parked on the side of the road, huge concrete pipes stacked next to it, in the shape of a pyramid. They'd paved most of the road again, the new asphalt black, the color of my Rorschach tattoo.

We kept walking and saw a man standing in front of a boarded-up storefront. He had an acoustic guitar with two strings. He wasn't playing any chords, just beating on it and singing at the top of his lungs. Not singing, exactly. Shrieking. He was squealing a John Lennon song that my mom used to sing, but he did it in such a way I never wanted to hear it again.

"Do you think that's a sign?" I said.

"It's definitely a sign," little-Rhonda said. "It's a sign that guy needs singing lessons."

TELL YOU MORE

Sometimes she'd come in my room at night and lie down with me. We'd stare at the ceiling and have the same conversation an infinite number of times. A conversation that always started with her saying, "Why did you do it?" and I said, "Why did I do what?" and she said, "Why did you destroy my body?" and I said, "I didn't destroy your body," and she, crying, said, "You destroyed my entire life," and I, crying, said, "How did I destroy your entire life?" and she said, "Why did you do it?" and I said, "What did I do?" and she said, "You destroyed everything," and I said, "How did I destroy everything?"

And now I'll try to tell you the story that she told me. The story of my birth. The day her life changed and she never forgave me.

My mom and my dad were not married, but lovers. They lived in rural Minnesota. Summer of 1976. On a commune. They lived with about forty other people. My mom was a classical pianist. An amazing classical pianist. She was nineteen years old. Getting ready to study music in college. I don't know where. She never told me that part. The point is she had a gift, and her piano playing was the thing she loved the most in the entire world.

The day I was born, they played gin rummy on the commune. My mom felt her first contraction. She said, "He's coming," because they knew I was a boy, and my dad went and got her suitcase and pulled the car up to the house, and he helped her into the car. They drove to the hospital. While they drove, he said, "We still haven't picked a name," and she said, "We've narrowed it down to three. We'll know which one is right once we see him," and he said, "I love you," and she said, "I love you, too," and they drove to another town in rural Minnesota, to the tiny hospital. He helped her inside. He went to park the car. He came in to meet her. She was in some pain, now. "What does it feel like?" he said, and she said, "You don't want to know," and the nurse said, "You haven't seen nothing yet, honey," and my mom forced herself to smile, but she didn't want to smile. My dad stayed right with her. Nurses smearing my mom's belly with an ointment and huddling around a monitor. Nurses pointing at the monitor. Nurses whispering to each other while pointing at the monitor. One nurse saying, "Go get him," and the other nurse ran out of the room, and my mom said, "Is something wrong?" and the nurse said, "Don't you worry," but she was worrying, she'd seen the panic on their faces and she grabbed my dad's hand and said, "Tell me everything's going to be okay," and he said, "I promise everything is going to be okay," and the other nurse came back with the doctor. They huddled around the monitor. Pointing and whispering. My mom and my dad holding hands. More whispering. The doctor said, "Your baby is backwards," because my feet were facing down like landing gear, and my mom said, "Is he safe?" and the doctor said, "He's got the umbilical cord twisted around his head and we're worried it might slip around his neck," and my mom said, "Oh, my god," and my dad said, "What can you do?" and the doctor said, "We're going to perform a C-section," and my mom said, "Oh, my god," and the doctor said, "We do this all the time. Nothing to worry about," and he left again to get ready for the surgery. The nurses left, too, one of them telling my parents they'd be right back. My mom said, "I'm scared," and my dad said, "I'm here." The next minutes had somehow cut themselves up into years. My parents held hands and kept saying, "I love you," and my dad smoothed her hair back and promised that everything was going to be all right, that he wouldn't let anything happen to her, and one of the nurses came back in and showed my mom a piece of paper, and the nurse said, "Is this your blood type?" and my mom said, "Yes. AB negative," and the nurse frowned and left the room again. My parents fought through the agonizing creep of time. My mom said, "Will you tell me a joke?" and my dad racked his brain to think of anything besides his girlfriend, his boy, the C-section, but he couldn't think of anything, and she said, "Please tell me a joke," and he said, "Did you hear about the pirate movie?" and she shook her head, and he was just about to tell her the punch line when the doctor and the two nurses came back in. The doctor said, "There's a situation," and my dad said, "What?" and the doctor said, "We don't have any AB negative, and we need blood to perform a C-section." My dad said, "How can you not have her blood type?" and the doctor said, "We've already dispatched an ambulance to St. Paul. It will be back as fast as humanly possible," and my mom bawled, and my dad said, "What do we do until then?" and the doctor said, "We make sure the baby doesn't start coming out," and the nurses shut my mom's legs and one of them said, "She's almost fully dilated, Doctor," and the contractions, an onslaught of pain, not even coming in waves anymore, but a pummeling of violent sensation. My mom crying so hard. My dad crying, too. My mom saying, "I'm going to die," and my dad saying, "You are not going to die," and my mom saying, "Our baby is going to die," and my dad saying, "Our baby is not going to die," and my mom saying, "Let's pick a name," and he said, "Now?" and she said, "Now," and they said all three names and talked about what they liked and disliked about each, and they picked my name.

Three hours later. My mom screaming. Sobbing. Three hours of her body being fully dilated and trying to push the baby out, but the nurses kept the baby inside. My mom thinking that this was so much pain, too much pain, and that she must be dying.

She said, "Good bye. I love you," and my dad said, "You are not going to die." Three hours later and my mom asked my dad, "What about the pirate joke?" and he said, "What?" and she said, "What's the punch line?" and he said, "The movie is rated AAArrrr!" and she said, "I love you," and she closed her eyes and didn't say anything and my dad thought she'd died. He pounded the side of the bed, but the nurse said, "She only passed out," and my mom didn't wake up again until after the C-section was over. The blood made it from St. Paul. The doctor cut her belly and yanked me out and we were both alive, and my parents were so happy, so relieved. Hours later, my mom fed me and my dad sat next to us, and my mom said, "My hands feel weird," and he said, "I'll get the doctor," but it wasn't for weeks of this buzzing in her hands, weeks of her fingers being clumsy on the piano that she went and saw a specialist who said, "You have rheumatoid arthritis," and my mom said, "I'm only nineteen," and the specialist said, "Body trauma," because she'd told him about my birth. The specialist said, "Trauma can trigger rheumatoid," and my mom said, "Well, what can I do?" and he said, "We'll do our best to relieve any discomfort," but this was the seventies, the decade where hospitals didn't stock AB negative blood, and they couldn't do much for her arthritis. She spent hours at the piano. Her fingers throbbing. She'd play for so long she'd cry, but she never played right. Hitting the wrong notes. Her timing off. The specialist gave her painkillers. She took a lot of painkillers. She was always taking painkillers and trying to play the piano, and my dad would say, "Snap out of it!" and she'd say, "I love the piano," and he'd say, "You love him, too," pointing at me, and my dad would say, "Get your head together," because he was frustrated with all her crying and painkillers and awful concerts. And everything floated out of my mom's head, everything except the knowledge that she'd never be a concert pianist and that knowledge was like a splinter rammed under the skin, the knowledge made her take more painkillers and drink tcha-bliss and shove my dad out of her life, and she was stuck with me, and I was the thing that had ruined it all. Maybe I was the splinter: this breathing crying whining eating burping puking pissing shitting splinter that reminded her of everything she'd lost.

So she'd come in my room. Sometimes every night of the week, depending on how much pain she was in. She'd come in and say, "You destroyed my entire life," and I'd say, "How did I ruin your life?" I think I always asked because I couldn't believe she really blamed me. But she did. She does. Still. She's somewhere right this second blaming every flickering misfortune of her entire life on me.

This is the nightmare I have, the one I didn't want to tell you about earlier. Except in the nightmare, I am not inside of her, I am standing where my dad did. We are in the hospital room, waiting for the blood, and I am standing there watching my mom endure the agony, watching her whelp and scream and cry, and there is nothing I can do to help her. I stand there, totally powerless. In the dream I say, "I'm sorry I ruined your life," and she says, "Why did you do it?" and I say, "I didn't do it on purpose," and she says, "All you had to do was come out headfirst and this never would have happened," and I say, "I didn't have any control over that," and she says, "It's all your fault," and I say, "Please don't say that," and she says, "Everything is your fault," and I say, "I'm so sorry," and I say, "I'm so sorry," and I say, "I'm so sorry," and I say, "I'm so sorry," and then she shuts her eyes and they never open up again, the only eyes that open are mine as the dream makes me panic and sit up in bed, my heart hitting the bones of my ribcage, in a frenzy like an asphyxiating fish.

THE STRONGEST GOD IN THE SOLAR SYSTEM

I slept on the burned couch. In the middle of my nightmare, I felt someone touching my hair, but I didn't open my eyes. "Mom?"

"It's me, Crash Man," old lady Rhonda said. She sat on the edge of the couch. "I still have a key to your place from your trip."

I opened my eyes. "Is your husband gone?"

"He left," she said, and I scooted my body so my head rested in her lap. She said, "I'm so sorry," and I said, "What happened?" and she played with my hair, saying, "We'd been married a long time and needed to make sure we were doing the right thing by splitting up."

"You weren't happy."

"Yeah, but there's nothing scarier than changing your life." She leaned down and kissed my forehead. "He and I were up all night talking. I need to take a nap, but I wanted to come down and let you know he's gone."

"Thanks."

"Thank you," she said, "for everything." Old lady Rhonda looked tired. Her long gray hair crusted along the edges of her face with dried sweat. Maybe tears, too. "Do you have plans tonight?" her fingers still working through my curls.

"No."

"I'd like to take you out."

"Where?"

"It's a surprise," she said, reaching in her pocket and handing me my wallet. "Sorry I took so long getting back to you." She winked at me. "Don't worry, I didn't steal anything, but I did learn some interesting stuff about you."

"Like what?"

"You'll see tonight."

———

A couple hours later, I looked out my window and saw three construction workers shoveling piles of hot asphalt on top of the dirt trenches. Another man, sitting on a bulldozer, waited to run it all over and fill the gaps.

———

Old lady Rhonda and I cut down 20th Street, passing Folsom. It looked like we were heading toward Damascus. I asked, hoping I was only being paranoid.

"It's a surprise," she said.

"I don't want to go there."

She stopped walking; I stopped, too.

"I looked in your wallet," she said, "and saw your driver's license."

"So?"

"So I know your real birthday is this coming Sunday."

Me, Rhonda, good hand getting the microwave-popcorn-feeling. Me, wanting to run away from her, humiliated, disgraced. She was the only person who had been nice to me, and I lied to her and for what, what reason did I really have?

"I'm not mad," she said.

"I'm sorry."

"Don't worry. But I organized a little party to celebrate the actual day. I'll be visiting my sister in Portland this weekend, so I thought we'd have the *soirée* tonight."

"I can't go in there," I said, imagining the angry sneer on

Vern's face, remembering the way he'd stormed out of my bathroom that night, repulsed and disappointed.

"Please. Let's go in, and if you're not having fun, we can leave. But please try."

I agreed because I didn't know how to say no to her, but Damascus was the last place I wanted to go. I felt true shame over the night with Vern and his tire iron, enough shame to make me never want to see him again. The same breed of shame I'd felt for the thousands of ways I hadn't protected my mom over the years, all the ways I'd done nothing to help her, all the days, months, years I'd thought about trying to contact her but couldn't bear the thought of her shunning me again. Shame is the strongest god in the solar system.

But I guess that's not really true. Shame can't be the strongest god, because I was ashamed of what I'd done, but I went into Damascus anyway. Old lady Rhonda asked me to go, and I did, so shame didn't wield as much authority as what I felt for her. What I still feel for her.

"Why do you want to throw me another party after I lied to you?"

"You should know by now," she said.

———

We walked into Damascus, into its outer-space paintjob. Back by the pool table was a banner that said *Happy Birthday*. There was a cake on a table.

Vern and Enrique were at the bar, drinking warm ones. I didn't want to talk to them, but old lady Rhonda told me to go say hi, she'd come in earlier that day and invited them to the party.

Vern eyeballed me as I walked over. I wondered if he'd told Enrique what had happened between us.

"You better not offer to suck off your commanding officer again," he said.

I nodded.

"Ever!" he said.

I nodded again: "I won't."

"Then happy birthday, Gunnery Sergeant Fellatio," he said.

"Thanks."

"Happy birthday, kid," Enrique said. "Two birthdays, pretty good trick."

Old lady Rhonda walked over to us and said, "Are you playing nice, Vern?"

He made a farting noise, little white tongue waggling again. "This lady," he said to me, "drove a hard bargain. Told us if we didn't come to your party tonight there'd be hell to pay, and the look in her eyes said she meant business."

We all laughed.

"Can we cut the cake?" Enrique said. "I'm starving."

"Let's have a couple drinks first," old lady Rhonda said, and we did. Enrique played lots of songs on the jukebox, most of which I didn't know, obscure rock and roll. Old lady Rhonda and Vern shot a game of pool; I sat and watched their flirty squabbling.

Out of the corner of my eye, I saw a bright light over by the bathroom, coming from little-Rhonda's helmet. He waved me over.

"Gotta go to the little boys' room," I said.

"Don't fall in," old lady Rhonda said.

"Or offer anyone a blowjob," Vern said.

"How dare you speak to him that way!" she said to him, menace in her eyes.

"Kitty got claws," he said, menace filling his eyes, too. "I like that."

She sighed and took her next shot on the pool table, six ball all the way down the rail.

I followed little-Rhonda into the bathroom, locked the door, and asked, "What are you doing here?"

"Finally celebrating the real thing, huh?"

"Can we talk about this later?"

"No, we can't."

"Why not?"

"I'm here to say good-bye."

"What?"

"I'm leaving."

"Where are you going?"

"Take your shirt off," he said.

"Why?"

"Just do it."

I pulled my shirt over my head and set it on the counter. "Why did I do that?"

"I have to go home."

"Where?"

"Jesus." He shook his head.

"Tell me."

"You still don't get it, do you?"

"Get what?"

He poked his finger into the middle of my Rorschach tattoo. His finger didn't stop at the skin. His finger moved right into my body. It didn't hurt, didn't feel like anything. Little-Rhonda said, "You didn't let Vern break your arm. The old lady loves you. I can go back home," pushing his arm farther into me, all the way up to his shoulder.

"You kept Vern from breaking my arm," I said.

"So did you."

"No, I didn't."

"Yes, you did."

I backed away from him. His arm slipped out of me. I covered my chest. I pressed my hands against the tattoo, to see if I could travel in there, too, but all I felt was the boundary of skin.

"Why are you leaving?"

"You don't need me."

"Yes, I do."

"No, you don't."

"How do you figure?"

He walked to me. He moved my hands away from my chest. I tried to fight him off, didn't want to let him go, but he overpowered me, like he'd done as he dragged me to the dumpster. "Hold still," he said.

"What if I need your help?"

"I'll always be helping you."

"What if I want to talk to you?"

"Then talk to me."

I didn't know what to say, tried to stammer a couple sentences, but little-Rhonda held up his finger. "Let's not draw this out," he said. "I don't want to watch you blubber like a baby." He put both his hands through my tattoo and used his arms like someone doing the breaststroke to open the tattoo wider. He stretched it until it was the size of a manhole. I wish I could explain to you what it felt like, but there's nothing to explain. If I hadn't been watching him do it, I'd have had no idea he touched me. His arms pried me open farther and he pulled his feet up off the ground and began to shimmy inside. His helmet disappeared into my chest, and little-Rhonda's face was about to slip into me and he said, "Well, this is it," and I said, "I'll miss you," and he said, "You can't miss yourself, Rhonda." Then he sank the rest of his head into my body. His legs stuck straight out of me, and I panicked, thinking that I'd never see him again, and I grabbed his legs, trying to keep him from going any deeper. I held him still. I wondered about my heart, wondered where it went while little-Rhonda slipped deeper into my chest. He yelled from inside, "Let go," and I said, "I don't want to," and he said, "You have to," and I said, "No," and he said, "Let me go." He kicked his feet, and I tried to hold onto him, please believe me that I tried to hold on, but I lost my grip and his body kept noodling, now burying his torso in. I watched as his back sunk deeper into me. His waist slipping in, his thighs, knees, calves. The last thing I saw of him was a ratty pair of sneakers, and then they were gone and he was gone.

My hands touched my tattoo, to try and feel the hole in my chest, but all I felt was skin.

———

When I walked out again, old lady Rhonda said, "Now who wants some cake?"

"I'm starving," Enrique said, and I said, "Me, too," and Vern said, "You know what, I'm damn hungry myself," and she said, "All my boys are famished tonight."

We gathered around the cake; it had white frosting and writing across it in bright orange icing, the color of Home Depot: *Let's start from scratch.*

"Thanks for doing this," I said to old lady Rhonda.

"Once I go on 'Wheel of Fortune,' we'll be set for life."

At first, I didn't say anything, thinking about me and old lady Rhonda, being set for life, having a life together in the first place. Then I said, "Do you really think so?"

"We'll either be rich and happy, or poor and happy."

She lit the candles. I put my face right over them, feeling their heat and taking a huge breath, blowing them all out.

"What did you wish for?" old lady Rhonda said.

But I didn't have time to answer her, because seconds later, the candles lit back up. I took another big breath and blew again. Some of them stayed out, but some came back to life.

Old lady Rhonda laughed and said, "Trick candles!"

We all cracked up.

"Come on, soldiers," Vern said. "He needs reinforcements," and they circled around the cake, the trick candles, circled around me, and all of us blew and blew until we'd finally put them out for good.

Apologies

This is supposed to be an Acknowledgements section. But I have this theory that anyone you wish to "acknowledge," you probably also owe an apology, even for the most prosaic crimes and intrusions. So here's my litany in no particular ranking of indictments. First, my dad. He's dead, and I was a smug little prick most of the time we knew each other. I hope he knows I'm not as smug or as little or as much of a… well, two out of three ain't bad. To my younger sisters, I apologize for a lack of latitude in my guidance; I probably should have pandered more than corruption. So it goes. I did the best I could with my contorted sensibilities and will hopefully learn to nurture you in better ways. My mom: I'm sorry if people think the mother character in this novel is you. Trust me, it isn't. This is fiction; this is a cluster of lies; no reason for Ms. Mohr to suffer the consequences for my sordid imagination. My ex-wife, I guess the "ex" makes this one self-explanatory. Mistakes were made… moving on. My step-mother, I'm sorry my dreadlocks gave the whole family lice while I was in high school. To every proprietor of every bar I flung drinks in: I drank on the job. I drank a lot. Really. It was ridiculous. I owe each of you like $20,000. To every ex-girlfriend for every set of sheets I soiled. To the selfless teachers in my writing life – Susan, Kate, Andrew, Dodie, Dan – I know I pestered you congenitally, but there were questions that needed answers, damnit, answers! Old roommates, yes, your accusations were all true. I stole CDs and drank your booze and played grab-ass with your significant others. To my favorite drinking buddies: Shana, Veronica, Marc, Matty, Jen L, Stix, Andrew B, Rick, Rob B, Michael A, Michael L, CY, Aubs and Pep, Ro and K: "To livers aching like shin splints!" Everything I've ever said to any of you in a blackout cannot be used against me in a court of law. To Eric and Eliza at Two Dollar Radio, a preemptive apology: I haven't known you long enough to do anything extraordinarily insipid, but it looms. To Amy and Robyn, I'm sorry if my insomniac emails ever made your jobs more trying (You try entertaining yourself at four a.m.!). And finally to Leota Antoinette: this isn't an apology, you don't need one; this is solely thanks for your resilience and advice and optimism and thoughtfulness and rousing heart.